DEATH IN THE DESERT

R.L. COFFIELD

OTHER TITLES BY R.L. COFFIELD

The Ben Thomas Trilogy:

Northern Escape, Book I

Murder in Thomas Bay, Book II

Death in the Desert, Book III

Nonfiction:

*Life Was a Cabaret: A Tale of Two Fools, a Boat, and a Big-A** Ocean.*

One Pot Galley Gourmet

You Can Conquer TMJ: Ideas and Recipes

DEATH IN THE DESERT

Printed in the United States of America.

Published by:

Moonlight Mesa Associates, Inc.

18620 Moonlight Mesa Rd.

Wickenburg, Arizona 85390

www.moonlightmesaassociates.com

ISBN 978-0-9774593-3-9

Library of Congress Number: 2008904856

10 9 8 7 6 5 4

Dedicated to Joanie Starr

May your "Starr" forever shine.

THE BEN THOMAS SERIES:
BOOK III

DEATH IN THE DESERT

A Story of Revenge and Reconciliation

BY R.L. COFFIELD

Introducing Arizona Marshal Jake Starr

MOONLIGHT MESA
ASSOCIATES

"What are the roots that clutch, what branches grow
Out of this stony rubbish? Son of man,
You cannot say, or guess, for you know only
A heap of broken images, where the sun beats,
And the dead tree gives no shelter, the cricket no relief,
And the dry stone no sound of water. Only
There is shadow under this red rock,
(Come in under the shadow of this red rock),
And I will show you something different from either
Your shadow at morning striding behind you
Or your shadow at evening rising to meet you;
I will show you fear in a handful of dust."

T.S. Eliot
The Waste Land, 1922

Chapter One

THREE sets of eyes followed Ben as his horse worked its way in the searing heat through the brushy terrain. The air scorched his throat, with the desert floor raging at 140 degrees. Even the horse, an Arab bred to withstand the rigors of the desert, sweat profusely as it ambled slowly, only its alert ears twitching. Man and horse felt staggered by the enormous weight of the sun beating down, a force that squeezed the breath from the body and slowly, excruciatingly, crushed one to death. Did it matter if he found the body of another dickhead drug peddler tied to a saguaro being pecked and scavenged by vultures? He'd be the one being scavenged if he wasn't careful. Dumb idea to ride into this area looking for bodies. There were probably hundreds that were only skeletal remains in the torpid furnace. Some actually mummified after the dying men crawled to the shade of thorny mesquites or greasewoods. His goal was to find them early on – before vultures, coyotes, and the scorching sun took their toll, when they might still be identified.

The horse halted abruptly and snorted dryly, its ears erect. Ben wiped the sweat from his eyes and looked about. He could see nothing but heat waves undulating above the sandy soil. *What a hellhole*, he thought. *Who the hell would be out here? Only an idiot*. Then he laughed silently. "Guess I'm one," he murmured.

Horse and rider remained riveted, and for a split second he felt the hairs on the nape of his neck rise in warning. It was too quiet, and too hot. He'd come back – maybe in the winter. Resolved to leave and to later return, he tried to relax, but an eerie shiver, a warning really, again coursed through him. He felt watched. Yes, someone was watching him. He could feel it now with certainty. The horse sensed someone too.

***

Five feet from the rider, Juana Antonia Rodriguez Salcedo huddled beneath a large greasewood. Her eyes, dull and vacant, stared at the man. In her right arm she cradled her dead daughter. She'd kept the baby alive as long as possible with the milk from her breasts, but the infant had died a few hours ago, the tiny child's angelic face upturned, with swollen tongue protruding through puffy, black, split, bleeding little lips. The baby had died in silence, looking to her mother with a questioning longing. She'd tried to smack her dry, cracked lips, but the swelling and the heat had robbed the baby of even the energy to breathe.

Juana's son lay sprawled across her lap. He, too, had died in the torpid afternoon heat. He'd whimpered a bit, his large brown eyes anxiously searching hers for a sign of relief. There'd been no tears from the dehydrated child. Heat stroke claimed him before the swelling and choking had. His soft, black hair lay matted and tangled. With her free hand Juana picked ants from his thick, dark hair, and savagely pinched each ugly, red ant in two. Could she pinch herself in two she would have done so. With each ant her hatred of the man who'd thrown them from the truck grew. She envisioned plucking out his eyes. Slicing his shriveled, stinking organ off. Urinating in his face. Hatred kept her alive even as she prayed for death.

She watched the rider. He could save her. But the two lifeless little bodies weighed her down. She tried to open her mouth to call out, but her voice, strangled by her dry swollen throat, uttered no sound. Her jaw moved, but her tongue prevented opening her mouth wider. Wearily she closed her eyes, but always she saw the hateful face of Bill Passkey, the man who'd dumped her and her children in the thicket of greasewood and cactus when he'd seen the headlights from immigration patrol vehicles. "Sorry, *puta*," he'd said, using the vulgar expression used only by ruffians and pimps. "This is where you get off. Maybe next time." She'd looked at him questioningly.

"*Que pasa*?" Her eyes widening in fear.

"What's happening, darlin', is this is the end of the road for you, so get the hell outta my truck." He leaned across her and opened the truck door, shoving both her and Carlos out of the vehicle with his foot. "Here, catch. Keep your papoose too," he snarled as he half-tossed the sleeping baby to her.

Juana's heart beat furiously as she stood under the Arizona night sky, watching the play of headlights from immigration vehicles fanning out in several directions. She'd been warned, true, but the man had seemed like her ticket out of the abject poverty and damnation she'd been born into. She only wanted her children to have a chance at life, and she wanted to salvage what she could of hers. As she stood under the brilliant stars, her future had never seemed more hopeless.

She held Carlos by the hand as the small boy quietly cried. The man's boot had bruised his little ribs. He wanted his momma to hold him, but she held the baby who also began to fuss. "Hush, *nino*. Let us hide. Tomorrow we will walk to a city. Tomorrow you will see an American city. You will go to school. We will live in our own house. I will find a job where I do not have to…" here she stopped. She'd spoken aloud mostly to calm herself, but Carlos, no matter how young, should never hear that his mother worked as a whore.

She could not remember not being a whore. From an early age she'd been used by men…as her mother had. She couldn't go back to that. Better to die here and now, and so she slowly began to let herself slip into the sleep of death when once again the "coyote's" face appeared before her. "Bastard! I will live to kill you!" She saw the man's heavy boot ruthlessly kick the fragile ribs of her beautiful boy. Juana Salcedo groaned in despair.

Her father had deserted her and her mother in Nogales when she was a toddler. He'd taken them there from Mexico City in hopes of crossing the border to obtain work, but at the last minute had left the young mother and toddler, vowing to send them money or to return for them once he was established in America. A proud young man, he resented his lot in life, of having to live in a cardboard shanty on the outskirts of Mexico City, never having a steady job, seeing his woman look at him questioningly every day, wondering if he'd be working that day or not. He grew to hate the beautiful girl he'd impulsively impregnated, and when Juana was born, he grew even more taciturn and increasingly violent. The tiny baby's existence in the hovel with the tin corrugated roof and dirt floor only reminded him of his failures.

Juana's mother, deserted, destitute and desperate, turned to prostitution to support herself and her baby. Uneducated, alone and virtually living in the streets, she'd done what she needed to survive. Juana, raised in the backrooms of a whorehouse, had been forced early on into child prostitution.

Abandoning her reverie, Juana gently stroked the faces of her two dead babies. At least they would never know the degradation, humiliation and shame that she'd known. Perhaps this was for the best. Her brain on fire, she wanted only to die. She didn't know that she lay only a hundred yards from where her father had perished from dehydration and heat stroke in the Arizona desert in his desperate attempt to save himself and his hapless little family.

***

Ben's neck appeared in the crosshairs of the scope of a second watcher. "Shall we blow your head off? Or blow it apart?" And the shooter raised the gun slightly until the side of Ben's head moved into focus in the crosshairs. A feeling of power surged through the rifleman. It thrilled him to hold a man's life in his hands, and his fingers lovingly caressed the trigger. "Maybe I'll shoot your horsey dead from under you," and he smiled as he targeted the Arab's stately head. "Eenie, meenie, minee, moe…" Bill Passkey laughed, excitement almost choking him.

Wait! The little whore! She was down there somewhere in those bushes, and he momentarily wondered if she was still alive. Such a pity to waste such a sweet piece of ass, even if she did have two bastard kids. He'd planned on leaving the brats off in the desert or selling them in L.A. anyway. His interest was solely in the slight, shapely young woman he'd seen in the whorehouse in Nogales. Unable to take his eyes off her, he'd whispered of a great life in America where he'd assured her he could find a placement for her as a domestic working in a mansion. He'd given her 500 pesos, 50 dollars, to dance naked before him. He knew it was a fortune for the girl, and when she complied and blushed in embarrassment he'd gone wild with desire. He could not tear his eyes from her lithe, slender body, a body that showed no signs of having borne two children other than her slightly milk-enlarged breasts, and he'd cried and moaned helplessly as he buried his head in her lap. "Bitch," he now said through gritted teeth, thinking how he had succumbed to her undulating body. Now who was in the position of power? Sweat dripped irritatingly into his eyes and he lowered the gun while he uselessly wiped his eyes on his sleeve.

He'd paid $1,000 to Julio Allegro Valdez for the girl, and now he was going to lose his investment because the goddamn immigration cops were crawling all over the Arizona desert. When he raised the gun again, however, he stared in astonishment and began to chuckle. "Can it get any better?" he spoke only to himself.

Now facing the shooter and looking nervously about, was his nemesis, the man Bill Passkey held personally responsible for bringing him down from his federal DEA job and foiling the largest drug smuggling operation in North America. "My good buddy Detective Thomas. Long time no see." Passkey studied the cop intently. "You get a break today, detective. 'Cause when I kill you, you're gonna know who's doing it!" He lowered the rifle a final time and walked heavily to the waiting truck.

***

Yet a third set of eyes watched the unfolding drama. Atop a neighboring ridge another man studied the desert floor and its occupants far below, including the mesa to the right where a white pickup with Mexican plates had only minutes before spewed out a decidedly Anglo-looking, heavy-set male armed with a hunting rifle. The cowboy intently watched as the armed man took aim at the rider below. He scrutinized the hunter's surreptitious stalking and wondered if this had been the same renegade and truck he'd seen the night before as it bounced across the rugged landscape, stopping briefly, then lights extinguished, continuing in the dark. He thought it might be. Obviously, something was down there in those bushes. Were both men looking for it? He wasn't sure. He'd seen the rider advancing for several hours, seeming to be looking for something.

"So. I suppose I'm gonna have to take you down, mister, if you shoot that rider," Jake Starr muttered to himself, pulling his rifle from its scabbard. Starr knew the rider below well – everything about him. For months he'd watched him searching for bodies in the desert.

Starr liked the cop. Liked his style. Liked his horse, even though it was an Arab. He himself had a bent for Quarter horses. He'd have liked to have had a drink with the man, for Starr knew he'd like him as a friend. He was tough. Honest. Starr felt relief when the hunter returned to the pickup and pulled away, leaving a visible trail of dust for the world to see. He saw the cop glance up at the dusty maelstrom the truck's departure created, then he saw him dismount and study the ground.

***

Below, on the desert floor, Ben stood looking at the sharply defined vehicle tracks and the less obvious passage of small feet. He couldn't actually see a footprint, just a tell-tale pattern of disturbed sand. He stooped and tugged at a small, red piece of cotton cloth caught on a cholla. It was not sun bleached. It was new. Perhaps the scuffle marks and shawl fabric had come from the same person.

He was too hot to think clearly. He should've seen the tire tracks immediately, but hadn't until he dismounted. True, it was possible they belonged to immigration officials. They'd been scouring the area, but Ben didn't think so. The tracks were wider than immigration vehicles made. These were not jeep tracks; these belonged to a truck. He squatted to study the sandy ground but the heat emanating from the earth almost devoured him. It was the blast of a furnace whose breath seared the air. He stood quickly, feeling light headed. He couldn't handle this. He'd go back. No dead body was worth dying for, he told himself. He looked at the sweat soaked horse before him and felt pity. He resolved to walk until he found shade. Horse and rider would return to the waiting truck and trailer when it cooled. Ben had seen an area at the foot of a mesa that offered a modicum of shade, and he started in the direction of the boulders strewn about the base of the slight overhang.

It was then that he heard a tiny, broken noise. It wasn't a desert sound. It was not the shrinking of the dry, crackling bushes. It was a human sound. Again. This time a bit louder, and he turned to the shrub. As he peered into the small space beneath the thorny bush he saw a pair of dull, lifeless eyes. She lay against the base of the shrub, her hair tangled in the thorns, her face scratched and bloody. On either side of her lay a small, motionless child.

"Jesus," Ben groaned as he stood and studied the fiery red ball overhead, still far from setting. She was alive, of that he was certain. She wouldn't live much longer, and he was certain of that also. "Jesus," he repeated. He reached for the phone on his belt and hoped like hell he got reception. These weren't the bodies he'd been looking for.

She was scantily clad, and Ben assumed she was a "working" girl. He guessed she'd probably been conned into crossing the border with the promise of a good job as a housekeeper, movie star, or whatever the girl wanted to hear. He'd seen far too many young women who grabbed onto any lie that offered them escape from the whorehouses and bars filled with men too willing to debase themselves and the women who serviced them. "Border whores" were the favorite targets of these exploiters of young women.

Death, hatred and fear mingled in her eyes. Momentarily he wanted to cry when he saw the hopelessness of the girl and her dead children. One look at the small boy told him the child had probably died of non-exertional heatstroke, something the elderly, chronically ill, and very young died from. The child's dry mouth and tongue indicated he'd suffered from severe dehydration which had undoubtedly caused his blood pressure to plummet, with death quickly following.

Ben could not remember when he'd last wept, but he could feel empathy for the plight of the three. Their stories were all the same. He'd seen it over and over and over until he was sick of the inhumanity that raged around him on a daily basis. Use. Abuse. No future. Nothing but despair, disease, poverty and death. The two lifeless little bundles beside the girl had probably been spared a life of misery by dying so uselessly in the desert. Their death was undoubtedly a blessing. He'd seen children in Mexico wandering the streets much after dark, selling packets of gum and other useless trinkets. For these children there were no bubble baths and bedtime stories. Early on they knew only a life and drudgery and scrabbling for bits of happiness, succumbing to the hands of strangers in back alleys for a few extra pesos and watching tall foreigners look through them as though they did not exist.

***

The cowboy on the hill watched as Ben reached gently to pull a half-dead female body through the thicket, and to load her and two dead looking infants onto the back of the Arab. He watched as Ben led the horse and its passengers a mile through the scorching sun to the shade shared by scorpions, snakes and spiders. Jake Starr dismounted and settled in to keep an eye on them until help came or until Ben made it back to his rig. Starr had work to do, but it would not be until later that he would begin. Yes, until then he'd just keep an eye on them.

Chapter Two

DETECTIVE Ben Thomas studied the stack of folders before him. Thirty-four in all. He had no doubt whatsoever that all thirty-four murders recorded in the files were committed by the same person…or people. It was possible there was more than one perpetrator, but he didn't think so. He sensed that a vigilante was at hand, methodically stalking his prey and leaving murdered bodies tied to cacti. Sometimes bodies were thrown on the more obnoxious, lethal looking plants and had to be ripped or pried from the long, dagger-like thorns. In every case the cause of death was the same: an acute overdose of the chemical the victim seemed to be transporting. Drug theft and gang retaliation were not the issues here, because the victim's smuggled supply was always left by the body. This was vigilante work, pure and simple.

Despite the reality that everyone secretly applauded the self-appointed, anonymous deputy of the desert, murders could not be ignored, no matter what kind of benefit the deaths might be for the rest of society. Like clockwork, every week for the last eight months, murdered people had been found throughout the Southwest. Hundreds of other bodies were found too, but the others had obviously died of heat stroke or dehydration. The thirty-four folders on his desk were strictly murder cases. Mexican authorities, alarmed at the deaths, were putting pressure on the State Department to stop the slaughter. "Must be cutting into their profits," Ben mused, immediately regretting his lapse into such nonprofessional postulating. No matter, a special task force had been formed to investigate what were now being called "The Cactus Murders." So far only two officers were assigned to the investigation. Internal Affairs carefully scrutinized those it assigned to the job. He knew that the possibility of there being a "law enforcement officer" vigilante was being quietly discussed among those in the know.

Circling buzzards and vultures marked the spots. It was important to arrive as quickly as possible before extensive damage was done to the corpses, but he no longer volunteered to ride out to the locales. His last foray had netted a pathetic, young Mexican girl and two dead infants. He'd investigated many deaths over the years, but his discovery of Juana Salcedo and her two children had done something to him – something irreparable. He wasn't sure he could go on facing the death and despair his job demanded. He no longer enjoyed the chase and the hunt with the old gusto. Instead, he dreaded looking into a killer's eyes. More than once he'd seen that familiar flicker when he looked into the mirror. He was haunted more and more by the demons of those he had put away or helped send to their deaths.

"Ben, you look so serious. What's up?" asked Chloe Littlebird, former Alaska State Trooper, currently employed as a private investigator. She frequently worked with him, and now stood in the doorway.

He gave her a token smile and tried to brush off his feeling of doom. "So, how was the vacation?" he asked, observing her tanned face and sun-bleached hair. Obviously she hadn't gone to Alaska as she'd led him to believe.

She faltered. "Ben, I…"

He knew it. Abruptly he stood and gathered the folders, turning his back to her. It'd been obvious to both of them when Chloe'd flown to Phoenix for extensive physical therapy two years ago, at his insistence, that their relationship would never get launched. His six-year-old daughter had taken one look at the woman and had loudly announced that she hoped Chloe wasn't thinking of staying. Shock had rippled among the adults present, but there it was. The child refused to apologize or to acknowledge Chloe again. The little girl then began an exhaustive campaign to find a new wife for Ben.

"Ben, we really should talk about this."

"Nothing really to talk about, is there?"

"Well, what's the problem then?"

"I was under the impression you were going to Alaska to see your family."

"I never told you I was going home."

"You told me you were going to see a friend. Obviously the friend does not live in Alaska." A moment of silence ensued and then he added, "How is Mack, anyway?"

As soon as he uttered the words he regretted it. He turned to apologize, but the doorway stood empty.

Well, what the hell else could go wrong today? Only one more item – the teacher conference at 3:00. Now what? He scooped up the folders and threw them into a briefcase. He'd study them tonight, although he already knew most of the material by heart. The hell with it. He tossed the briefcase under his desk, grabbed his jacket off the hook, and strode out of the office, angry at everyone, ready to do battle. He'd go golfing and hit the hell out of the ball…after the conference with Miss What's-her-name.

"Detective Thomas…yoo-hoo…" a female voice trailed off. He waved the voice away without turning around. He took the stairs to the parking garage, speaking to no one and ignoring all eye contact. His jaw set, and he knew his face was easy to read: BEWARE.

All the way to Wickenburg nagging thoughts of his job, his daughter and Chloe flashed through his head. Why was he so upset? There never was a relationship with Chloe really, only the possibility of one. She was still stuck on a guy whose ass he should have hauled off to jail, who was now living somewhere in French Polynesia, and Ben had a daughter who despised her. Not a good recipe for two people to get together. "Let it go," he told himself for the umpteenth time.

Then there was Stephanie, his ex-wife and mother of his daughter, who had recently moved to Phoenix, ostensibly to work in the district attorney's office. She'd stopped by to see him and to make arrangements to take Jere to some horse show, and he'd found his hands sweaty and his collar suddenly strangling him when she calmly greeted him as he sat in the squalor of his small office.

There was nothing between them except their daughter – who he had custody of. That the mother and daughter missed each other was painfully obvious to him, and he reluctantly relinquished more of his time with Jere so she could see her mother, which meant he had to talk with Stephanie more also to discuss arrangements, like pick-up times, recitals, and other small but important details that are involved in raising a child. The two had even sat together at Jere's first piano recital.

He wondered if Stephanie had been notified of the "emergency" parent-teacher meeting today. He dreaded these kinds of meetings and hoped she might be there after all. Maybe he'd need an attorney. She always remained so calm in the face of adversity and confrontation. For him, confronting a gun-wielding felon was a fact of his everyday life. Confronting a second grade teacher made him anxious and uneasy.

When he was honest with himself, he knew he was disappointed with Chloe because he'd been so wrong about his feelings for her. He'd acted impulsively and through emotion when he'd invited her to recuperate in Phoenix from the deadly wounds she'd received on a case he'd helped her with in Juneau. If he'd waited and thought things through he probably would never have invited her, but he had, and that was that. At first, after Jere's proclamation, he and Chloe had still enjoyed dinners and evenings out. As time passed, however, he found that, other than cop talk, they didn't really have much in common. She often seemed distant and distracted, and he never attempted to ignite any passion for her. Both seemed emotionally disconnected from the other. He fretted about his daughter's dislike of Chloe who in turn resented the child's demands on him. Then, when the ex-wife had appeared out of the blue, he'd seen the final curtain call of the relationship written on Chloe's face. When Stephanie had stopped by Chloe's office and introduced herself, Chloe had admitted to Ben that she had blanched uncomfortably before the cool, calm, collected and stunning ex-Mrs. Thomas.

He winced as he recalled Stephanie's account of her conversation with his "dumbstruck, little police friend."

"I thought I should introduce myself since our paths might cross from time to time," Stephanie recounted to him. "After all, I'll be picking Jere up regularly, and I don't want any unpleasantness to occur in front of her."

He knew, and was certain that Chloe knew also, that things would never work out between the two of them. After Stephanie entered Chloe's office, he saw that there was no mistaking that Chloe had heard the funeral dirge of their floundering relationship. In that instant, he had to admit what he'd always known unconsciously. There was only one man for her, and it was not he.

"To hell with her and Mack both," he consoled himself as he roared up the 101. "They deserve each other." He sighed and turned his attention to the freeway. He'd jump onto the 17 and head up to the 74 and cut over to Wickenburg that way. His motorcycle, capable of speeds up to 180 miles an hour since he'd installed the turbo a few years back, took off like a small rocket and he settled down to focus on the traffic and his driving.

Thirty minutes later he parked in front of the elementary school. Straightening his tie, he walked into the building as though he were hearing his death knell. He knew the location of the classroom – this was not his first "urgent" conference. The last time had been a year ago when he'd been called in because Jere had handcuffed and roughed up a boy. She had a strong sense of justice, and often enforced her own law and order when she didn't feel that the proper authorities were responding correctly. The teacher hadn't appreciated him showing up in his SWAT gear and had insinuated that perhaps Jere's troubles stemmed from his own obsession with violence. That had undone him, and he'd left the school in a rage after storming the principal's office and scaring half the office personnel to death. Stephanie had handled the other two conferences, much to his mixed consternation and relief. Obviously this new teacher hadn't heard about him or she wouldn't have called the meeting.

Miss Johanson, a petite, attractive blonde, nervously rose from her desk to greet him. "Detective Thomas, please come in and have a seat." Despite his best efforts, he could find no chair appropriate for his size.

"Forgive me. Here, use my chair," the young teacher said, blushing.

"Thanks. So, what seems to be the problem here, Miss Johanson?" He wasn't in the mood for pleasantries.

"I so appreciate you coming in during your work day. I told Jere that I could meet with you at night, but apparently she never told you I wanted to see you."

"Is she in trouble or something?"

"Detective, I don't know any other way to put this, so I'll just come right out with it: your daughter is obsessed with finding you a wife. I don't know if you know it or not, but I've caught her several times visiting dating services on the classroom computer and entering information about you. Last week she ordered a small bouquet of flowers to be delivered to your ex-wife for her birthday and had the florist sign your name."

"How the hell does she pay for all of this?"

"I'm afraid she's been using your credit card."

He sat, stunned into silence. Now it suddenly made sense why his junk mail folder on his home computer had lately been filled. His eyes nearly popped from his head when he instantly understood the reason for the increased female traffic strolling past his office door, the friendly smiles and nods, the "yoo-hoo" voices and the continuous hubbub around the water cooler. Good crap! He had to look like the village idiot of the department. He could see Linda whats-her-name smacking her spinster lips and it gave him the willies. He'd probably be invited to be a guest on some salacious talk show next. He slowly shook his head, "Thank you for bringing this to my attention. I'll speak with her about it."

"I just thought you should know. I've caught her several times using the computers for this purpose. I hate to forbid her to use them, but it's against school policy for the children to use computers for anything other than educational purposes."

"I understand. Do what you have to do. I'll speak with her." He rose, not certain what more needed to be said. Then, "Does Jere's mother know about this?"

"Yes. I thought I should tell her about the flowers and…well, you know. I didn't want there to be a problem for either of you because of it."

"Good. Well, thanks. The problem will stop, I assure you. Anything else?"

Did Miss Johanson hesitate, or was he simply antsy to escape the scrutiny of the young woman? Before she could reply he abruptly lurched towards the door, curtly nodded, and fled the room.

What a totally screwed up day, he swore silently to himself as he strode purposefully to the motorcycle. Jere had unwittingly exposed him to who knew how many ex-cons who might be gunning for him, and who knew how many psycho women who looked for love in the wrong places. Even worse, she'd put herself and Francesca, their long-time housekeeper, in jeopardy. What would possess the child to do such things? Flowers to the ex-wife? Matchmaking services? Frustration surged through him. He'd never lifted a hand to Jere, but now he understood the maxim, "Spare the rod and spoil the child." Being a parent was becoming the most difficult part of his day. Golf balls weren't going to do it. He needed a punching bag.

He fired up the V-Rod and headed to the health club, with visions of thirty-four dead bodies, Juana Salcedo, Chloe, and Jere manically racing through his mind. Maybe Stephanie was in the concoction also.

Chapter Three

BILL Passkey sat at the bar enjoying the cool evening breeze and watching the flow of tourists as they paraded up and down the colorful, bustling streets. He had a meeting later with Miguel Lorenzo, and Passkey needed time to prep himself. Things were going better than he dreamed, and he wanted more of the take. He smacked his lips in greedy excitement. The dumbshit cops had fallen again for one of his ploys. He was a genius, pure and simple. While the cops were turning their attention and resources to the border and the dead drug runners, he was sending tons of drugs to the states via the airlines. While customs officials and airline security were busy harassing teens and retirees, no one ever thought to inspect the planes themselves. It was genius, that's all there was to it. No one closely observed the baggage handlers, fuelers and other personnel as they prepared the scores of planes that left San Jose del Cabo every day of the week. TSA were too busy trying to check dirty laundry in luggage, sifting through plastic bags of tourist mementos, collecting meaningless paperwork and keeping computers running.

Lorenzo didn't see the big picture, instead lamenting loudly over losing the runners who were sacrificed for the plan. And at first Passkey himself had been furious, but he quickly realized that the dead runners, each carrying relatively small amounts of drugs, were the cost of doing business. The Americans thought they were stemming the flow of narcotics when they discovered the dead, but they were only running all over the Arizona desert rounding up hapless illegal immigrants and working themselves into a dither over a few expendable low-level "mules." Passkey was mildly curious as to who the vigilante was who was offing the unfortunate peddlers and decided he should probably make it his business to find out – retribution and all that, but for now he just had to explain to the stupid beaner Lorenzo that the dead bodies were good for their business, that it kept the Americans looking in the wrong places, that it was a hugely helpful diversionary tactic. He knew, thanks to the inside snitch, that the State Department was involved and that a special task force had been assigned to investigate the murders. Idiots. All idiots.

So, he would meet with Lorenzo and patiently explain to the greasy Mex why the dead drug runners were helpful. Look at the bottom line, Lorenzo, Passkey thought to himself. He'd insist that Lorenzo tell his people that he wanted more of the cut, or he'd pull his connections at the airport and go independent. He knew that was not a good idea, for he was on their turf, but he could threaten all the same, if he had to.

Passkey looked around, admiring the young girls and their suggestive flirtations. Easy pickings this week, he decided. Must be spring break…or some other college holiday, for there was a plethora of young action around. Mmmm mmmm. He'd score tonight. Get one of these gals drunk and he could do anything he wanted when they saw the roll of bills he'd pull from his pocket. None of them compared to the little Mexican whore he'd lost, but a few would do.

Now the little Mexican gal was another story. He'd have to find him another one, but he knew from experience it'd be a while before he found one the likes of Juana What's-her-name. He swirled his quickly warming beer around the glass and raised his eyebrows to the bartender, signaling for another.

It'd been seven months since he'd dumped her and fled from the border patrol, if memory served him. He assumed she was dead. Had to be since she never showed up again at the whorehouse in Nogales. *Nada*. He'd searched for her for several weeks, waiting for the INS to escort her back across the border, but nothing. He'd head back that way his next trip to the states and check again, just to make sure.

But for now, he was living the good life in Cabo. His passport, one of many false ones he owned thanks to his past position in government, had expired, but a fist full of pesos turned any Mexican cop's head 180 degrees. So, here he was, a fugitive going under the alias of Bill Villanova, residing just north of Cabo San Lucas, keeping what he considered to be a low profile. It beat the hell out of a federal penitentiary which would now have been his permanent home had the cops in Alaska had their way, especially the asshole from Phoenix. He'd never figured out what the hell the Arizona cop had been doing in Alaska anyway. He'd get the bastard eventually -- probably should have brought him down last fall in the desert. He kicked his own ass every time he thought of the perfect shot, the perfect murder he'd let slip through his hands, just like the 200,000,000 dollars that had slipped through his hands in Alaska, thanks to the detective's uncanny abilities.

His iron grip on the glass tightened as he unconsciously ground his molars in fury. When Miguel Lorenzo tapped him on his burly back, he almost erupted.

"Hey, man, be cool. It's only me," Lorenzo said.

It was a second before he could respond. "Yeah. Right. Let's talk over there." He nodded towards a table in the corner. "Two more." He slid the bartender ten dollars and steered Lorenzo to the darkest recess in the room.

***

Juana Salcedo gazed out across the pristine, groomed beach and deep blue sparkling sea, beginning again to see beauty where for months she'd seen only darkness and grief. Had it not been for the kind policeman who'd saved her life in the scorching desert, she might well have ended it, but his efforts deserved better than that. His kindness still brought her to tears, and she shook her head, blinking quickly to stem their flow as she turned to vigorously wipe down the marble counter in the guest room at the resort where she now worked. She had him to thank for the job also, and she blushed in gratitude as she moved her cleaning supplies to the waiting cart.

Carefully she surveyed the suite, checking each room again to be certain that everything was in perfect order. She was more than thankful for the job, even though the pay was meager. Sometimes the guests left her tips, and she carefully hid this money in a sock in her cardboard nightstand. She knew what she would use the money for, but could not yet think such thoughts.

She paid her cousin, with whom she lived in a one-room slump block shack down a back street of Cabo San Lucas, one hundred pesos – ten dollars – a week. That left her just enough for food, clothing, and a very few amenities. The one-room abode had no bathroom other than a pit in the small backyard where she showered in tepid water that dribbled from a hose coming from a roof cistern. She managed to keep herself and her uniform meticulously clean, despite living in a casita with dirt floors and dusty streets. Her cousin, a former prostitute her mother's age, lived with an unemployed guitar-strumming singer and worked selling trinkets to tourists.

Juana knew her rent money was helpful, although the lack of privacy for all was often a source of difficulty in the one-room dwelling. But for Juana, anything was better than the Nogales whore house and the bitter memories that arose when she thought of her life there. She'd finally accepted that she would never be able to shake the image of the tragic faces of her dying children, and so she settled into the small barrio house and tried in vain to find what peace she could. Not a day passed that she did not remember the tragedy that befell her in the Arizona desert.

For a week she'd hovered near death in the American hospital. Finally, the day came when an agent arrived to escort her to a holding cell where she would stay until she was bussed back to Nogales. It was then that the policeman who'd rescued her arrived. She remembered every detail, every nuance…

"I'll take Miss Salcedo back," Ben announced when he walked into the room.

"And who might you be?" the agent, miffed, asked.

"Detective Ben Thomas, Phoenix P.D." came the authoritative answer as he flipped open his i.d.

"And what, may I ask, is your interest in Miss Salcedo?"

"I'm the one who found her and her…" Ben hesitated. "I found her."

"Well, I'm sorry, but this is not proper procedure. She'll have to go with me."

"Where are you taking her?" Ben demanded, clearly annoyed.

"She'll be where we take all the illegals…are you sure you work here?"

Ben fumed. He turned to Juana, and in his broken Spanish tried to explain to her that he'd see her later and take her to Mexico. Juana wanted to smile at his efforts, but she burst into tears instead, throwing herself at the feet of the INS agent, begging to see her babies. Since neither Ben nor the agent spoke Spanish well enough to understand her, the agent pulled her up by the arm saying, "There, there. You can go home in a few days."

Two days later, when Ben came to escort her from her cell, he could see surprise flash across her otherwise stony visage.

"This is highly irregular, Detective. Make sure you get signatures verifying that this Mex here actually crosses the border, or your ass is grass. Don't think about taking her home to be your maid, if you get my drift," the INS agent looked warily at the cop and the attorney standing before him. Ben nodded curtly, took the paperwork and escorted Juana from the building.

He'd asked Stephanie for help in getting the young woman released and had been surprised when she took time from her crushing schedule to accompany him. He was astonished at his ex-wife's fluency in Spanish as she asked Juana where she wanted to go, explaining to her that she had to return to Mexico, but maybe Nogales would not be the best city. The two women talked quietly for some time before Stephanie patted the girl on the hand and turned to him.

"She'd like to go to Cabo San Lucas. She says she has a cousin living there she can stay with."

"What do you think?" Ben asked.

"I think she's telling the truth. She can't go back to Nogales."

"Can you get her papers to stay, Steph?"

"Sorry. She came illegally. She's got to go back and apply. She'll never be admitted. Not at this time anyway. Nothing I can do."

"Okay," he sighed with heavy resignation. "I'll drive her to Tijuana. Put her on a bus. Hope like hell she makes it."

"I'll take care of Jere for a day...until you get back."

"It's too far for you to commute to take her to school, Stephanie. Francesca can deal with her okay. That's what I pay her for."

"I'll stay at your house in Wickenburg – if you don't mind, that is."

He thought for a few seconds and realized it would be the best for Jere. He nodded his approval as she exited the car. "Thanks again."

"No problem." She turned to Juana and rattled off something in Spanish. The young girl nodded, smiled weakly and then immediately lowered her eyes.

Despite his efforts at conversation, the eight hour drive to San Diego was mostly silent. He could see that Juana, lost in her agony, was oblivious to his pathetic attempts at conversation. He knew that she didn't hear him, or maybe didn't understand him at all, as he labored to contact Hector Pinto, the manager at Playa Blanca, a resort in Cabo where he and Stephanie owned a timeshare that they now split between them, alternating years. Ben had spent many an evening bullshitting with Hector on his bi-annual vacation, and hoped the man remembered him well enough to give Juana Salcedo a job at his request. It was a terrific long shot, but the only idea he could come up with.

From years of experience working vice, he knew that Juana was expecting him to demand a sexual favor in return for his help, and he winced when he saw her looking at him questioningly. He knew she wanted him to speak to her, to assure her she was safe, that he would not hurt her, that he would not take advantage of her. But silly phrases like "I am fine. How are you?" kept running through his head. He promised himself he'd take some Spanish classes so that he could say more than *Dos cervecas frias* - two cold beers, and *dos mas*, two more.

Once across the border and papers for her deliverance signed, he secretively pressed a wad of money into her tiny palm. He smiled and told her in English to take care of herself. He wrote out Hector Pinto's name and number on a business card, telling her to see Hector for a *puesto* – a job – the word seemed to jump out of him. He didn't realize that Juana understood far more English than he supposed, and as he turned to leave he didn't see that she stood, momentarily stunned. Never had anyone given her anything without exacting something in return. He had just handed her a handful of American dollars and hadn't asked for anything. He'd saved her life once, and now, whether he knew it or not, he was saving her life again. "*Amigo*," he heard her whisper as he walked away. "*Amigo mio. Vaya con Dios*." He understood the phrases and smiled in gratitude, even though worry for her weighed on him...

Daily she replayed the scene of her deliverance. She lived, for now, because she owed the tall policeman with the soft brown hair and gray eyes. Even if he did not collect, she owed him her life. She would live for him so that his good acts were not a waste. It was sinful to waste good acts.

Two months ago she discovered that Passkey resided in Cabo San Lucas. She'd seen him as she walked down the hill to catch her bus after her twelve-hour shift. She could tell that he hadn't recognized her with her newly highlighted auburn hair. She stumbled and gasped as he drove by in his car, talking to a rich-looking American man.

For two weeks fear and anxiety gnawed at her. Terrified that he'd see her and recognize her, she began wearing scarves and sunglasses. But after two weeks she began to unwind as she saw the beauty of her situation. He must assuredly think her dead, she reasoned. She would be alert now that she knew he frequented the area. She'd be on the lookout, and eventually she'd find him and murder him in his sleep, even if it meant that she had to debase herself again. As her fear evaporated, her hatred grew. She had now found another reason for living.

Juana tried to hide the strange, sly smile that she knew came over her face from time to time. Finally, she hid her emotions no more. Let her cousin think what she would, for she knew that the older woman already thought her a foolish young girl who would not last.

Chapter Four

HIS temples throbbed and his jaw ached from the strain of trying to keep his calm while he'd been verbally pulverized by Phillip Dowling in front of the Special Task Force. Dowling had been brutal in his assessment of the lack of progress in the Cactus Murder investigations. Ben couldn't brush Dowling's curt barbs aside as he usually did. He heard his heart pounding in his chest. His head ached, and he felt nauseous...and helpless.

"Detective, your phone's ringing. Would you like me to answer it?" Dina Woodruff's head poked through the doorway, interrupting Ben's nightmare trance. He glanced up questioningly.

"Your phone, sir?"

"Right. Thanks. I'll get it." He watched the secretary's head slip through the narrow door opening. He could almost hear her breathe a sigh of relief. He knew that when his face wore "the look," it terrified her.

"Thomas here," he growled into the phone, not caring who was calling for what.

."Ben?"

"Yeah."

"It's me...Stephanie. Are you okay?"

"No. I'm not," he responded more curtly than he intended.

"We need to talk, Ben. It's important."

"Yeah, well I already heard what a dipshit failure I am. I got that one loud and clear."

"Don't beat yourself up until we talk. When are you free?"

Curiosity began to tug at his morose state of mind. “As far as I’m concerned I’m free now. How about you?”

“I have a 2:00 meeting. How about 3:30 at Angelo’s?”

“That place over in Tempe?”

“Yes.”

“See you there. 3:30.”

He stared at the phone after he hung up. Bewildering and perplexing thoughts began building. Stephanie had been at the morning meeting, which surprised him in some ways. In fact, a trio of attorneys, he assumed all from the D.A.’s office, had been present, and at the time he vaguely wondered why, but he’d been distracted by the hullabaloo that ensued. He didn’t recall seeing them at a Task Force meeting before. He knew Stephanie had been to a few, but in truth he hadn’t ever paid a lot of attention to other attendees. This meeting caught his attention, however, because he’d been targeted and caught unawares.

It was a long four hours until he met her. Too much time to leave early and to wait, not enough time to accomplish a lot in the office in the mood he was in, not that he felt like doing anything anyway. Hesitantly he picked up the receiver and punched in a familiar number. With each ring he barely resisted the temptation to hang up. By the fifth ring he was preparing to do so when the recognizable voice answered.

“Hi. Chloe? Yeah. It’s me, Ben.”

There was an icy pause. “Yes. I know who it is.”

“Yeah. Uh…” He fell silent, wishing he’d not called.

“Well?”

“Are you still wanting to work with me on the Cactus Murder thing?”

“You hired me for it, Ben. If you recall, you even gave me a retainer.”

"Well, I didn't know if you'd want to work it after...you know...after what happened in my office the other day."

"Would you like your retainer back?"

"No. No, actually I need some help."

"What's happening?" It was helpful that she was all business – at least on the phone.

"That's the problem. Nothing's happening. I've scoured the area on horseback, by jeep, copter, dirt bike, quad, and on foot. Nothing. Yeah, I find dead bodies now and then, but I'm getting nowhere as to who's doing it."

"Well, I've had a bit of time and done some sleuthing." Both tried to laugh at this long standing joke between them. After an outing once into the desert around Wickenburg, he began calling her the Desert Sleuth after she pointed out numerous signs and tracks that he'd been completely oblivious to. He argued that her observational skills and tracking ability had to be inherited from her Tlinkit Indian ancestors.

"So, what have you sleuthed?"

"Well, now that you ask, some very curious things have turned up. When do you think we can talk?"

He was about to say now, but instantly remembered his meeting with Stephanie. He wanted to say tonight, but...maybe the meeting with Stephanie would linger. He suddenly realized that he was hoping it would.

"How about tomorrow morning?"

"Sure. Let's meet for coffee. Better yet, can you just swing by my place? I have some stuff I want to show you."

"Okay. 9:00."

"Trying for banker's hours?" Chloe asked. He detected a note of surprise in her voice.

"Right."

"Bring some donuts, will you?"

"Right. See you then."

He hung up and, glancing at his watch, decided there still remained too much time to leave for his meeting at Angelo's. He'd study maps. He liked maps, and he'd amassed a stack of them since this case had started. The most intriguing one, however, was tacked to the wall with almost forty colored pins sticking in it, each representing the location of a dead body found roped to a cactus. The pins were color coded according to the drug the coroner found in each body's organs. The pins were beginning to spread, with the last two in the Wickenburg area, quite a distance from the border. The dead there, however, were not illegal immigrants who died on the hot, long desert transit. Rather, these victims were known for drug peddling and trafficking. Each had a rap sheet, prints on file, a mugshot, and a bad reputation.

Their manner of death was the same as that of the migrants found farther south, however. Loaded with their own narcotics, the bodies were left tied to cacti, usually a saguaro. He was stumped. Despite hours on the internet and in the records room, he could find nothing that stood out. His usual ability to find a word, a sentence, the smallest detail that led to a solution, seemed to have escaped him. Normally, he gleaned massive amounts of information surfing the web. He possessed an uncanny knack for entering the right words into the search engines. Not this time. Whoever was doing the murders was methodical and dedicated. He felt certain that the culprit worked alone and had a personal motivation – maybe one as simple as the death of a loved one. He was willing to bet on it.

He pulled the obituaries again. He kept a small box of clipped obituaries that he'd had Dina Woodruff pull from newspaper microfiche going back for ten years. He searched for deaths that resulted from drug overdose. This required locating police reports, pathology reports, and so on. It was highly labor intensive so far with poor results. Since many people don't even have obituaries, it became necessary to check death records in general. He had Dina pull the names of everyone under the age of forty who'd died of drug related causes. It was a massive assignment, and he doubted she was equal to the task. Weekly he took a couple dozen from the boxes on the floor of his office and personally reviewed them. He'd found a few oversights and that made him nervous.

A question began to loom. What if the murderer was a person of influence who might have squelched an autopsy report? Maybe what he should be doing was looking for deaths of a suspicious nature that had no accompanying police report on file. He needed more clerical help, that's all there was to it, but how could he ask for any after his recent berating? He made a note to talk with Dina about missing reports. He'd target only victims aged twelve to twenty-five.

With that, he settled back in his chair with a stack of folders before him and began reading. He was looking for a young death, no reports. Maybe an influential name would pop up in the process too.

***

Chloe Littlebird hung up, suddenly realizing that she was holding her breath. A flood of emotions swamped her, and she bit her lip in an effort to keep herself steady. She knew he'd call eventually, but it didn't help matters that he actually had. Don't fall to pieces on me now, she chided herself. Think, girl, think.

She'd done nothing but think, that was the problem. For the last year she'd spent every night thinking of Ben and her predicament. Obviously the relationship was over. What little of

Ben she'd had melted to nothing once Stephanie Thomas reappeared on the scene. Chloe knew better than to try to compete with the mother of Ben's child. It was never going to work. She knew it, and she knew it was time to move on. That was the real problem though, wasn't it?

She needed to talk with him. She craved his "blessing." For some silly, girlish reason, it seemed important to her. She, who didn't take a back seat to any man, now waffled in the decision of her life because she needed, desperately, Ben's approval. If he would just give her the nod, she'd be gone in a heartbeat.

She picked up the picture on her desk that'd been taken just a few weeks ago. She couldn't believe how happy she looked in the picture, and how miserable she felt now. In the photo she stood, with Mack's arm securely around her shoulder, on a pristine white beach, palm trees in the background. Both of them wore smiles that melted her heart. She could feel the heat from the coral beach and the tropical sun overhead even as she studied the photo.

Her resolve began to return as she smiled at the man in the picture, the man who had left her in shambles, turning her almost perfect life into bedlam. She would bring her business in Phoenix to a close and go back to Papeete. There was no reason for her to return home to Alaska. She would never be able to return to law enforcement after the injury she'd sustained in Juneau, thanks to Bill Passkey, the crooked DEA official, and his tribe of henchmen. Had it not been for Ben, the case would never have been solved, but then maybe she would never have been injured.

"Stop it!" she ordered herself. That part of her life was completely over, and she had to come to terms with it once and for all. And she did have Ben to thank for rescuing her from the pity-party that she'd begun wallowing in while recovering in Juneau. But, despite her fondness for him, there was really only one man in her life, and though she'd tried valiantly to make her relationship with Ben a go, it was now obvious to her that she'd been seeking to forget Mack, not to love Ben. Mack, the love of her life who'd ended up betraying her with his dishonesty. She wanted to point fingers at everyone, but she knew that had she done her job thoroughly, in the very beginning, none of this would have come to pass. None of it. It was almost too painful to admit, especially in the dark of night when she laid alone, her injured back aching, her heart torn in two.

Squaring her shoulders, she returned to the boxes sitting half-filled in the living room. She'd move them into the bedroom for now. No point in discussing things with Ben until after she helped him solve this one last case. Then she'd be on her way to Mack. She'd write him tonight, telling him of her one last job.

It was funny how things worked out, she thought as she stacked the boxes in her small bedroom. From the moment she'd laid eyes on Stephanie Thomas, she'd known that it was over for her and Ben. There was something about the woman's regal bearing that spoke volumes, and Chloe read it all in Stephanie's perfect composure. Stephanie had come to reclaim Ben, pure and simple, and he didn't even know what was happening to him.

Okay, let's get on with things, she encouraged herself. She pulled a file from the tall oak cabinet sitting by her desk and proceeded to the kitchen. She would review her notes and findings and let Ben take what he could from what she'd gathered. She hoped it would be helpful; the sooner he could bring the case to a close, the sooner she could get on with her life and, as Ben always put it, "get the hell out of Dodge."

Chapter Five

DESPITE his best efforts not to, Ben arrived forty-five minutes early for his meeting with Stephanie. He requested a corner table in the shaded courtyard where the overhead misters and brilliant bougainvillea combined to ease the tension squeezing his head and chest. After his first icy mug of beer, he loosened his tie and stretched out in his comfortable seat, half reclining, and began to notice the colorful courtyard filled with a variety of desert flora.

It was the clicking of high heels on the terra cotta tiled floor that brought him out of his reverie. Looking up, he saw Stephanie approaching, her willowy body and elegantly coiffed auburn hair attracting looks from men and women alike.

"Been here long?" she asked

."Nah. Not too long." He hoped the hostess had not revealed otherwise if Stephanie had stopped to ask for him.

"Good."

He rose, pulling out a chair for her. She smiled in return, and he felt a quiet ping in his heart. She still has what it takes, he thought. "Iced tea, please," she said to the waiter. "Want another beer, Ben?"

"Sure."

He watched her nod her assent and the young man left to fill the order. It was just like her to want to take charge. He smiled to himself.

Neither spoke for a minute, each wondering where to begin. "Well, you heard it from the horse's mouth today, Stephanie. I'm stuck. This investigation is going nowhere...and me with it." He watched her re-settle her purse and herself in her seat. He could tell she was stalling. As she'd intimated on the phone, had she planned on leveling with him about something, but now had second thoughts? He studied her face carefully. He saw the twitch of the eyebrow. There had to be a lot at stake for her to be so hesitant. He hoped that what she would tell him would not jeopardize the career for which she'd given up so much and worked so hard. He watched her refold her napkin several times.

As she met his eye, he could almost see her mind calculating in nanoseconds. He hoped she saw before her a man who had a sterling reputation as a law enforcement officer. The father of her daughter. Her former spouse. A man for whom she might still harbor a small spark of feeling.

He was being sacrificed, and he knew that she knew it. He prayed that in her heart she'd find the courage to offer him an explanation and a way to manipulate the situation. But Stephanie was not always about "heart," as he well knew. He understood that there were often innocent casualties when the government became involved in international espionage and intrigue. Would the fact that she now personally knew a victim make her question her fealty and commitment to the special task force? He hoped so.

He could only guess how much debt collecting from various colleagues and superiors she'd done to be named to the task force formed ostensibly to investigate the notorious Cactus Murders. Officially called Team Saguaro, the group consisted of too many attorneys, Mexican representative Michael Lorenzo, FBI officials, Jake Starr of the Arizona U.S. Marshal's Office, and Deputy Directory Marcus Elderberry of Homeland Security. It was a formidable group. He wondered how much she could reveal to him.

"You look serious, Stephanie."

"What I want to tell you is serious, Ben. Deadly serious. Do not doubt for one minute that if you breathe a word of what I'm about to tell you, that I'll be finished. Do you understand me?"

His affability quickly faded as he saw the deadly glint in her eyes. He nodded, his attention fully riveted on her earnest face.

"Ben, there are some heavy players on this task force. In fact, there's a whole other layer that you're unaware of. You've been under the impression that Phillip Dowling is just another busybody attorney, but in point of fact, he's DEA from Washington."

"Not another one of those assholes," he muttered, reflecting on his brush with Bill Passkey from the Alaska case he'd assisted Chloe with.

"I thought you'd feel that way after the Juneau episode."

"What the hell is going on, Stephanie?"

"Here's what you need to know, Ben. Don't ask me more than I can tell you. At least not now." She looked at him for agreement, and he reluctantly nodded."Okay. What I'm going to tell you will be hard for you to hear, but you need to hear me out and not have one of your shit fits."

He squirmed uncomfortably. She had a way of pinning him down that made him feel like a chastised child. "Okay. Shoot."

"Ben, the Cactus Murders are just the tip of the iceberg. Nobody really cares about the bodies being found in the desert. This is not the focus of the investigation. The right people, people like Dowling and Elderberry, are saying the right words to assuage the Mexicans, but no one, *no one*, cares about dead drug runners. The case is not the Cactus Murders."

"Then what the hell am I doing running around the desert playing cowboy?" He could feel his pulse quickening.

"You're doing what they want you to do. They can report to the Mexican government that everyone is working hard to find the murderer of these young men, but Ben, no one cares about the drug runners. The case goes beyond them. The Mexican cartel at the bottom of this thinks they are distracting us by sending the runners and that we are wound up trying to locate the murderer. You, however, are the only person really involved in the murders."

She paused to give him a moment to digest the information. "How well do you remember Bill Passkey?" she continued.

"I'll never forget that asshole."

"Did you ever see him, face to face?"

"No. I never did, actually. Don't tell me he's in on this shit."

"We believe Bill Passkey is the one sending the runners. He's doing it to divert our attention, and he thinks he's succeeding. But Bill Passkey – he calls himself Bill Villanova now, by the way – has wormed his way into the Vincente Bassili cartel."

"Never heard of that one."

"No, you wouldn't because it's new and it's quickly becoming our worst nightmare."

"It's out of Mexico?"

"It's out of Chicago…via the Mid-East and the Pacific Rim…via Mexico. Bassili was a nonentity until about a year ago. He appeared out of nowhere and is now an international person of interest. It seems he has connections to everyone, and no past."

"No, don't tell me Matsuya, or Miyaga or whoever it was in Juneau is in this one."

"We're not sure, but we know that Passkey is shipping over a ton of drugs to the states per week. His cartel involves Mexican officials at the highest level, and may involve American officials at the highest level too. Unbelievably high, trust me. That's why the secrecy and hush-hush. That's why, unfortunately, you are a cheap decoy for the real case."

He took it better than he thought he would. Hearing the words that he was expendable was a blow, but inevitable in his line of work. He leaned back, looked around, and ran his hands over his taut stomach.

"My boss wouldn't do this to me," he feebly protested, not believing himself what he was saying.

"No, your boss wouldn't under normal circumstances. He doesn't know the whole story."

After a moment of silence, he asked, "So what do you suggest?"

"Here." She slid a file folder over to him. "Solve the cactus murders. Take a leave. Take Jere and get the hell out of Phoenix for awhile. Go back to school. Get your Masters Degree in something and become a professor or something safe. Your metal work is beautiful, Ben. Take up art again."

"There gonna be fallout from this arrest?"

"More than you can imagine."

"Is it worth doing?"

"That's up to you. If you don't catch the murderer, you'll come under more and more heat. We have to keep the Mexican government appeased and off guard. If you do catch the guy, you become expendable. Many people don't want him caught. Either way, the situation isn't good."

"Isn't there any other scenario?"

"Yeah. I suppose you could resign."

"What about Passkey? What if I bring him down?"

"Almost impossible to do, Ben. He's living in Mexico, just north of Cabo San Lucas in fact. He has damn near a fortress and a small army protecting him, including Mexican and, we believe, corrupt American government officials."

Ben eyed the folder that still lay on his side of the table. "And the contents of this folder?"

"I've been led to believe that it *may* help bring the cactus murders to a speedy close."

"Just like that?"

"I hope so."

"How'd you get involved in all of this, Stephanie? Where are your ethics?"

"Don't get judgmental this late in the game, Ben. You are way behind."

It was out in the open now. She'd told him enough, just enough, but not the whole story.

"Tell me about Bill Passkey."

"Tough. Resilient. He'll stop at nothing to wage his own war against the world. It doesn't matter who the enemy is. I see him as an angry sociopath. Toss in the proverbial greed, lust, and self-loathing, and there you have it. Word is that he has you on his list for retribution since you blew open the case in Juneau." Stephanie paused, bit her tongue, but could not stop herself. "How's your little friend doing, anyway?"

Ben scowled in reply and ignored the barbed question. "So, let me get this straight. The folder will lead me to the cactus murderer?"

"I don't know, but I've been led to believe it may be a help. A big help."

"Who else is privy to this information?"

"Well, I only know of the person on the task force who gave it to me. There may be others, but I have no idea who." She still had not come up with a reason for Michael Lorenzo quietly handing her the folder after their last meeting.

"Jesus, Stephanie. I wish you could hear yourself!"

"Ben, you had better get this through that big, fat, thick head of yours. I scrambled to get on this task force precisely because of you. I was privy to a lot of high security information in Los Angeles, and what I heard scared me. Short of going to court for custody of Jere, the only thing I could think to do to keep an eye on my daughter, and you, was to get involved in this mess," she hissed. He could see she was resisting the urge to jump up and stomp away

Is Jere at risk?"

"For god's sake, Ben. You're a cop. Of course she's at risk. She's always at risk. Every time you arrest someone, or bring someone down, she's at risk."

He squirmed uncomfortably at her response. "Okay. Let's calm down, shall we? Let's just take things slowly."

"No, you calm down! I'm doing you the favor of your life, do you hear me? I'm putting myself and my career at risk. For you! So don't tell me to calm down, goddamn it!"

"Agreed. I'm calm, see?" He lowered his voice to a whisper.

She nodded curtly.

"Okay. Anything else?"

She shook her head no.

"Stephanie, thank you. I know you've taken a huge risk for me. I won't let you down."

"I appreciate that."

"Just out of curiosity, what would *you* like me to do?"

"What I want is immaterial. I just do not want my daughter to grow up fatherless. She dotes on you. You're all she can talk about."

"Stephanie, what *you* want is important to me. It's not immaterial." He blushed and hoped she didn't notice. He heard her sigh.

He had no idea that what she wanted was her ex-husband back, nor did he know that she had ruminated on their failed relationship for years, and that she had come to some brutal conclusions. He would never deny that he'd been obsessive with his job, but clearly she'd contributed to the demise of their marriage also by being petulant and demanding of his time. He understood that she hadn't been prepared to share him with a job that was all consuming. He disliked that she'd abandoned her own goals and dreams, and not at his request or urging. In fact, he'd encouraged her to go to law school, to pursue a career. Sadly, he had to admit that she'd had a child only to garner more of his time and attention. He'd grown sick of her pleading and cajoling him to return to private corporate security, ignoring the fact that he loved his job. She had, in effect, backed herself into her own corner and had found escape only by leaving. Pride had prevented her from calling and asking his forgiveness. Pride had kept her from admitting her decision was bad. Pride sat between them now. He felt miserable and alone as he watched her nervously rotate her glass of tea. He had no way of knowing that she yearned to take his hand in her own…but pride kept her hand planted solidly on the icy glass.

Finally, he reached over and took her long, slim hand in his. He held it briefly, and he could feel his warmth dissolve on her cold, wet fingers. He could not find the words he needed. Slowly he slid his hand from hers. He had no idea that it was all she could do to stop herself from reclaiming it. He stood up, gathering his coat and the file folder. "Can I walk you to your car?"

"I don't think we should leave together, Ben. I don't want to take the chance that someone might see us."

"Yeah. You're right, of course. Thanks for the heads up, Stephanie."

She nodded and watched him leave the courtyard, handing the server a twenty dollar bill.

"You are way too generous," she mused. "You always have been." Perhaps that was one of the things she loved about him…and missed.

Chapter Six

A full moon filled the November night, lighting the desert, causing shadows to cast themselves full length across the rocky terrain. A good night for hunting, he thought as he saddled the horse. He whistled softly, stroking the horse gently, talking quietly to the high-strung, nervous animal. "Hey, Buddy. You're looking good tonight. I'm counting on you." He continued in a lulling tone, steadily and quietly, and the horse slowly calmed. He didn't mind a spirited horse, but he needed composure for his expedition. This wasn't his regular mount. His usual steed still suffered from a stone bruise incurred on their last mission. He checked the horse's hooves. "You're gonna be needing some new shoes pretty soon, aren't ya?"

The soothing talk continued, and soon the horse and man melded as one. Both fiery natured, they held their fire in check. Later hell could be unleashed.

He set off in the mild Arizona night, the horse's hoof sounds only audible when rocks covered the path. The steed, at first snorting in excitement and some fear, quieted after twenty minutes, and the rider sensed the animal's muscles relax. He sank into the saddle more, and felt the horse's hips working beneath his. They moved as one, both alert, yet composed.

He would work south, for he'd heard there was feverish activity in the Organ Pipe National Monument. According to his source, large numbers of immigrants were scurrying across the border since the weather had cooled, weaving their way north through the cactus covered landscape. He didn't care about the workers coming to save themselves from their hideous lives on the other side of the border. He cared only about the handful of smugglers who came north with them. He cared so very much.

Over an hour passed before he came to the precise point he'd scouted days earlier. The tell-tale signs of heavy foot traffic, along with the remains of garbage, plastic water bottles, backpacks and other human refuse, declared unmistakably that travelers were afoot. Halting in the shadow of a tall organ pipe cactus, the rider silently watched the worn path. Within ten minutes he sensed the inimitable sign of quarry.

Hunched over from the weight of their packs, two young travelers moved noisily, eyes glued to the ground in an effort to avoid likely objects to stumble over. The trekkers didn't see the dark horse and its rider in the shadows. They heard only a whistling noise. One scampered quickly ahead, while the other stopped, straightened a bit, and peered into the moonlit landscape. The whistling grew louder. "What the hell…?" he spoke softly to himself. Suddenly, his head was snapped by a sharp, flying object. A second later he was jerked off his feet and pulled roughly over the prickly, rocky ground.

A scream instantly erupted from his throat as long, sharp barbs bit into his butt and legs. His arms, pinioned to his sides, kept him from grabbing the lasso and pulling himself upright. His only reprieve was the pack which partially protected his back and neck. Profanities billowed forth as he ground his teeth in agony. The pain. He couldn't take the pain a moment longer. Within minutes, screams turned to sobs and pleading, punctuated by outbursts of blasphemy.

The rider heard the young man screaming, but it didn't dissuade him from his course. He'd heard it before. They all screamed in agony. No one ever came to their rescue, so it didn't cause the horseman alarm or concern.

"Scream away, you bastard," the mounted man answered the wails of agony.

He dragged the smuggler far enough that finally the noise subsided. The rider knew that the human body could withstand only so much pain until it ceased to be felt. He stopped by a large organ pipe, its many arms lifting to the starry heavens.

"So, *amigo*," he said as he dismounted, leaving the lasso wrapped about the pommel of the saddle. "What'cha got for me tonight?" he asked in fluent Spanish. The young hostage opened his eyes, and the captor knew his prey was thinking he might be one of his own. Someone robbing him – someone betraying him. Maybe someone going to kill him as a warning to others not to tread into this territory.

The tall, well-built Anglo towered over the prostrate, whimpering youth. "Yep. I'm the gringo you've heard about; the gringo your *companeros* all fear. Those stories now roaring through your head? The warnings? Bet you and your friends sat around talking tough, bragging about what you'd do to the gringo if you ran into him. Where're your lousy, no-good, drug-dealing pimp friends now?"

The captor's unmistakable hatred blasted forth with each staccato word as he watched the prisoner lay with his head in the dirt, tears flowing down the boy's sweat-soaked, filthy face.

"You gonna die like a man or what?" the captor asked. When no answer came, the tall assailant shrugged. "Suit yourself." And he began untying the lasso from the saddle pommel, then expertly binding the weakened captive's hands and arms.

"So, what'cha got in your bag, partner?" he asked, squatting beside the quaking youth.

"Take it. Take it all. Just let me go." The hostage answered in a trembling voice.

"Nah. Don't be so selfless. You deserve everything you're gonna get."

Suddenly the hard sole of a boot crashed into the prisoner's face. The terrified young smuggler almost fainted in pain while he watched the man before him dump the contents of the pack onto the desert floor.

"Well, look at this. What's this now…meth?"

"*Si…meth,*" he whispered.

"Well, that's just grand. You ever tried this shit?"

"*Si…uno tiempo…once…only once.*"

"Well, that's good. You're gonna get to try it again then. Here. Open wide now."

Brutal fingers squeezed the prone youth's jaws open as the cowboy poured the contents of a bag down his throat.

The rider stood. Always a sick feeling overcame him as he watched the fear and terror in a dying man's eyes. He steeled himself as the young man before him convulsed after several seconds of gagging. The attacker knew death would follow soon enough. He re-tied the lasso and threw the line over the top of the cactus. Mounting his horse, he spurred the animal forward, slowly pulling the jerking body hard upon the cactus' needles, taking extreme care not to damage the plant.

"Good night, now. You tell your friends about me. You tell them to stay the hell out of my path. Out of my neighborhood."

He headed the horse back, knowing terrified witnesses watched from the shadows of the surrounding vegetation. He rode with impunity, as if daring anyone to step forth to defend their comrade.

Though his heart was heavy, he had lost the sensation of guilt. Killing did not bring pleasure for him. It simply brought justice.

He could tell by the moon's position that dawn was only a few hours off. He loved this time of day/night. It was cool. Calm. Quiet. He closed his eyes as the horse turned towards home. "You did good, Buddy. You did good." And he patted the sweaty animal. He refused to think of the young man dying in the shadows of a stately cactus under the canopy of stars above. Thinking would only cause regret. He had regrets enough already.

Chapter Seven

BY the time Ben arrived at Chloe's apartment, it was well past 9:00 a.m. He hadn't slept much the night before. Instead, he'd sat at his desk for hours after he'd put Jere to bed, staring at the unopened folder and going back over his conversation with Stephanie. As a cop, he'd been well trained in remembering and reviewing evidence. Once back at his bike, he'd taken a few minutes to record key elements of his conversation with Stephanie. He watched her leave Angelo's and climb into her Lexus, glancing about nervously as though looking for someone tailing her. When she saw Ben on his motorcycle, she smiled and gave a tiny wave. He nodded in return as she drove away.

If he opened the folder, it'd be all over. He'd have to arrest the Cactus Murderer, and he knew he would open the folder, no matter how long he postponed or argued with himself about it. That was his job. It didn't matter that the victims were running drugs across the Mexican border into Arizona. Could he convince himself otherwise?

At 4:00 a.m., still without answers, he dozed off. It seemed only minutes later that he vaguely felt Francesca covering him with a blanket. Then heard her rousing Jere and preparing her for the day, quietly shushing the loquacious child. He felt Jere kiss him goodbye as Francesca prepared to walk her to school. Despite the child's assertions that she could walk to school on her own, that she wasn't a baby, Ben insisted that she be escorted. Most days he drove her on his motorcycle, which thrilled her, but on those days when he couldn't, Francesca routinely took her.

It was past 9:00, almost 10:00, when he rang Chloe's doorbell.

"Well, good morning, sleepyhead," she greeted the unshaved, coffee and donut-bearing man in her doorway.

"Yeah. Good morning yourself."

"Problems?"

"Hmm. You could say that."

"Wanna share?"

He paused. He couldn't tell her of his conversation with Stephanie. Should he tell her of the folder which he still hadn't opened? "Not now. Later, maybe."

Chloe only smiled in response. Ben appreciated that she seemed to know that trying to extricate the information from him was hopeless. He could sense the pique in her curiosity, but he knew her police training would keep her from wheedling him. He also knew a cup of coffee and a foot-long maple bar would help appease her.

Neither spoke for a minute while he hungrily scarfed down two chocolate-covered donuts. He could feel Chloe studying him carefully, and he wondered what else was on her mind. There was definitely something in the air. He knew her well enough to detect her subtle signs of anxiety.

"So, whatcha got for me?" he finally asked as he drained his cup.

"Well, it may not be much, but I found a few interesting tidbits I thought might help you out." She left the room, quickly returning with yet another file folder. Sitting down, she opened it and looked through the pages without saying anything. Finally, she handed the folder to him.

"Want me to talk? Or do you want to read first?" she asked.

"Talk."

"Okay. Now this may seem unimportant, but...I was out in the area where a lot of the murders are going on. Just snooping around, you know? You gave me a retainer and I was proceeding even though at the time..." she paused. Ben said nothing, so she continued. "Well, I came across a small group of illegals, all of whom scattered when they saw the jeep. I stopped and started calling out to them, you know, telling them I wasn't INS, Immigration, *Policia* , etc. Finally, a young woman approached and asked for some water. Fortunately I had a case of it with me, and I gave all of it to the ones who came forward. We started talking, and did I get an earful."

"Okay. I'm hooked. That's against the law, by the way. Aiding and abetting," Ben added sarcastically. "Anyway, proceed."

"Well, I started talking about the dead bodies being found and that they should be careful. They knew exactly what I was referring to. Now, my Spanish isn't fluent, but I was able to piece together that the dead had been recruited by a man named Miguel Lorenzo who works for a big *jefe* named Villanova. It seems some are being paid, some blackmailed, to carry the drugs across."

Lights tried to flash in Ben's exhausted brain. No, couldn't be, he thought. Yet the odds of a different Miguel Lorenzo being involved on both sides of the border in the same case seemed remote. He knew Lorenzo to be a common name, however. Probably a coincidence, but one he'd remember to check out.

"How are they being blackmailed?" he asked, snapping his attention back to the conversation.

"I asked the same question. I guess a lot of them leave a wife and kids on the Mexican side. This Lorenzo threatens the family. Powerful stuff for these young men."

Another light flickered in Ben's sleep-deprived brain as he vaguely recalled Stephanie's account of Passkey now calling himself Villanova. "Well, son-of-a-bitch," he muttered.

"You know this guy?"

"Yeah. Villanova. And, I'm sorry to say, so do you."

"Villanova? I know a Villanova?"

"Try Passkey. Bill Passkey."

He saw her eyes widen and her face blanche.

"Not Juneau…not that Passkey."

"The one and the same."

He wasn't prepared for her reaction as she lurched from the chair and began pacing the room, wringing her hands. She stopped, pale and trembling, and he knew the memories of the Juneau case were cascading upon her. She looked deathly sick as she excused herself and ran to the bathroom.

Retching, sobbing sounds erupted, and he kicked himself for not thinking about what her reaction might be. Had he needed to tell her that Villanova was Passkey? Probably not, he thought as he reflected on the conversation.

What seemed an eternity later, she emerged, white and obviously shaken. He doubted she would want to stay on the case now that she knew her nemesis, Passkey, might be a player.

"Are you okay

Yeah. I'll be fine," she answered weakly.

"I'm sorry, Chloe. I didn't think."

"No. It's okay. I just wasn't prepared to ever hear his name again."

"Sorry."

"Okay, where were we?" she asked. He watched as she sank, exhausted, into her seat.

"You were saying that Villanova was behind the drug runners."

"Right. So I asked if they knew, or had heard anything, about the murderer. And one of them said yes, that his cousin had told him it was a man who had a big ranch in the Ajo area."

Well, that narrows it down to a few dozen anyway, Ben thought. "He didn't have a name, did he?"

"No. But he said that his cousin told him the man was *muy importante*."

Great, Ben thought. So no wonder everyone is afraid to move against him. "What else?"

"He just said that Villanova was the devil in the flesh and had killed and raped many women."

"Now how would he know that?"

"I don't know. Rumor. Urban legend. I'm not saying all this is true, but I got the information, I think, pretty much from the horse's mouth. And, quite honestly, if Villanova is indeed Passkey, is there any doubt?"

He nodded. Maybe what was in the folder Stephanie had given him would support the hearsay evidence.

"Well, I'll check out who holds title to land in that area."

"I already did."

"What'd you find?" Her energy and efficiency always amazed him.

"Look for yourself."

He spent a moment looking through the folder, scanning quickly. Suddenly a very familiar name caught his eye. No, can't be, he thought. But there it was, Jake Starr, head of the Arizona U.S. Marshal's Office and a member of the task force.

Don't get ahead of yourself, he reprimanded himself. There might be all kinds of important people who have property in that area. He scanned the few remaining names and saw only one other that aroused his curiosity, that being a member of the Arizona

House of Representatives. Maybe Starr was not even the one Chloe was thinking of.

He could feel her scrutinizing him and knew he'd have to give her a sign that he saw a suspicious name.

"So, which one do you think it might be?" he asked, hedging.

"It's obvious, Ben. Andrew Scott. It has to be him."

He almost breathed a sigh of relief. "And what makes you so certain?"

"He's the one backing all the measures to bring illegals to justice. He's the one who wants to build a wall along the border. It's his platform. What better way to push his ideas than to dramatize the issue by having the deaths all related to drug smuggling? He could run for governor or senator based on this propaganda. Probably even President."

Ben nodded his assent. "I'll check him out, but I think it's a long shot."

"Well, that may be, and I have my own doubts. Still, it seems a bit too coincidental that he has a huge ranch out that way and has such an overwhelming anti-drug, anti-illegal platform."

"Good job, Chloe. You've been very helpful."

"Do you want me to ride out with you?"

"Yeah. Next time I go out I'll give you a call."

"So. Okay then."

As he stood to leave, he could see she wasn't finished and was struggling with something. He waited momentarily, watching her screw up her courage.

"Ben, I'm leaving."

"Leaving?" He hoped his bringing up Passkey had not brought back too many agonizing, painful memories. "Another trip?" he asked, almost hopefully.

"No. I plan on leaving the area."

There was a long moment of silence.

"Oh."

"Well, is that all you have to say?"

He could not mistake the hostility in her tone. "Okay. I give up. What do you want me to say? You want me to beg you to stay? I can't, and you know it. We both know things haven't gone as we'd hoped."

"I know," she said, the sadness in her tone impossible to miss.

"I'm sorry, Chloe. I didn't expect Jere to respond to you the way she did."

"I know. And I know she's your daughter and she comes first in your life. But it isn't just Jere that's the problem."

He looked away, trying to avoid eye contact, knowing that what she was saying held more than a morsel of truth. Since Stephanie had come to Phoenix, things had turned even more cold and distant between Chloe and him. He hoped she would not drag Stephanie into the discussion, but he could see it coming. He tried not to wince.

"So, how's she doing, anyway?"

He ignored her question. "So, are you going back home? Or are you going to Papeete?"

It was out in the open now. He saw her falter.

"I haven't decided. I just don't think Phoenix is the best place for me."

"Nor is Papeete, living with a felon."

"I don't think that's really any of your business, Ben."

"You're probably right, but you need to think about who you are, what you stand for, and what he did." He hadn't intended to extend an invitation to argue and breathed a small sigh of relief when she didn't head in that direction.

"Anyway, I just wanted to let you know, as a personal and professional courtesy, that once we, you, close this case, I won't be staying around."

"You don't have to stay and help."

"Yes, I do. Particularly now that I know Passkey is somehow involved."

"Be careful. Don't do anything you'll regret. He's dangerous. You're too emotionally involved to handle anything remotely connected to him."

"I'll be careful."

"Don't make me have to come and arrest you," he tried to tease.

"Not to worry," she smiled unconvincingly.

He paused outside her door. Should he go back and talk to her? Try to convince her to stay? He knew there was no point. Their relationship was history – an empty history at that - still he felt a sense of responsibility for her.

He carried the file to his bike and placed it with the other as yet unopened folder. She was right, even though he could barely admit it to himself. Since Stephanie's return things had begun to spiral out of control for him. He found himself looking for chance meetings with her in the hallways of the legal system, checking for her car in the garage where he knew she parked, looking forward to her visits to collect Jere for their time together. She'd left him once, why would he go there again, he kept asking himself.

But there were little things he was beginning to notice. Her smile seemed to be for him only. Often their eyes met and lingered, like they knew what each other was thinking.

And then the kicker. It was her week for the time share that they split in Cabo San Lucas, yet she told him that she'd forgotten and had arranged for a condo at a nearby resort – did Ben want to use the condo while she and Jere were at their resort? They could spend Thanksgiving together, something Jere might enjoy, she'd hastily added.

It was becoming too complicated for him. Maybe he was just reading too much into everything. Cops did that sometimes, he reminded himself. He just might head into the desert tomorrow - to take a break from the wiles of these women, if nothing else.

As for Chloe...Ben revved the engine of his bike, trying to drown out the sound of his thoughts.

Chapter Eight

BILL Passkey, or Villanova – as he now preferred to be called – sat on the veranda overlooking the aquamarine majesty of the Pacific Ocean. He had it all, finally. Despite his setback in Juneau, things had worked out better than he could ever have imagined. Other than the fact that he had to be very cautious when he made his infrequent trips to the states and had to grease the palms of several high ranking Mexican officials, his life was sweet. And boring. Boring as hell. Despite his newly formed "friendship" with Vincente Basilli, a man who would make the smuggling life much easier, Passkey felt isolated. His Mexican cohorts largely shunned him. He was not a participant in their social milieu. In point of fact, he knew they despised him for his carnal incivilities and crimes. His stately and magnificently decorated hacienda echoed his solitary footsteps as he paced from room to room. His staff, largely cowering and shunning the sight of him, silently performed their duties, staying on the premises only because the pay was significantly better than they could get elsewhere. But there was no telling when the man would turn a vicious eye upon one of them. Turnover among the staff was regular, particularly among the young chambermaids and female kitchen help.

Despite his constant efforts, Passkey still could not satisfy the animal urges that raged in him since his time with Juana Salcedo. He could not erase the girl from his mind no matter how many other young girls he raped and sodomized. Once he thought he'd seen her in a crowded market in Cabo, but the hair was not the right color, yet there had been something about the set of the young woman's shoulders, the grace of her movements that had riveted his attention. Had he not been in his car at a crowded intersection he would have chased the girl down just to make certain.

Vincente Basilli would be en route to Cabo from Chicago in a few weeks. He had arranged for an equal number of young boys and girls to be present for Basilli, not knowing the elegant man's inclinations. A special menu would be prepared, and Miguel Lorenzo would be in attendance only because of the insistence of Basilli.

He rubbed his hands together in anticipation of the coming meeting. He'd orchestrated both ends, and had done a masterful job of it, he had to admit. Because of Basilli's connections, he now had the shipping transportation assured. And because of Lorenzo's Mexican connections, the airlifts were going perfectly. He couldn't believe that he could ship so much dope into the states and not saturate the market, but apparently the distributors were recruiting new users faster than he ever imagined possible. Everyone was getting rich, from government officials down to the street corner peddlers, and there appeared to be no end in sight, that was the beauty of it. What the hell did he care if it essentially crippled part of the United States of America, both financially and morally? He lived in Mexico, and he had already socked away enough to live in luxury in any country in the world – any country he could get into, that is.

Everybody involved was prepared to leave the U.S. when it entered its final throes of decadence and ruin. Enemies would point out that democracy had failed, but in point of fact, the country would have been brought down by the terrorism of Arab sponsored drug cartels and the greed of entrepreneurs like himself. The elusive Weapons of Mass Destruction were not nuclear missiles and chemically engineered diseases. No, the weapons of mass destruction that so useless a war had been waged over grew in poppy fields around the world, fields that the United States government unwittingly subsidized. And the ingredients for the worst weapon of mass destruction, meth, could easily be purchased in drugstores, hardware stores, and farm supply.

It was the perfect ploy - bring the United States down from within. And the beauty of it for him would be that it would take years – years in which he could live in luxury and hedonistic abundance. Who cared what happened after he died?

Even as he considered his growing empire, he busily calculated how many partners he could take out of the picture in order to increase his revenues. His rapacious greed knew no bounds, and as he finagled, his urgent need for violence mushroomed. Maybe he and Basilli could off someone during his visit. He didn't know Basilli well – he'd have to be careful.

This would be a perfect time, however, for a crime. The streets of Cabo would be glutted with throngs of tourists. It might be days before the police took action on a missing person report. Thanksgiving was a big week in Cabo. There was not a room to be had in the city. He knew, of course, that messing with the dollar-laden tourist industry was dangerous. The *policia* would only turn their heads so many times. Cabo must not get bad press.

***

Vincente Basilli gloomily looked out at the ponderous, charcoal-colored clouds that filled the Chicago sky. A bone-chilling wind blew off the lake, and he knew from experience that not even his cashmere-chinchilla blend overcoat would keep him warm when he left the penthouse. He hated this godforsaken landscape. The ugliness of endless skyscrapers sat in stark contrast to his memories of the wide, heat swept expanses of Saudi Arabia. He easily recalled sitting in his long jellaba, sipping thick, heavily caffeinated coffee with his uncle, the flaps of the tent gently rippling in the hot desert wind. The two men, at peace with the desert beauty, talked and philosophized for hours. Here, here there was endless chatter and grating noise, poisonous smells in the air, chemicals in the food and water, and everywhere decadence and decay.

His business in the United States would soon be concluded, however, and he would return home, but only after he met with the heinous American in Cabo San Lucas. Never had Basilli, born Mohammed Ashcraf Oman Farooqui Rhizouli, met such an unsavory, despicable, loathsome individual. No wonder the United States of America was flushing itself down the toilet, into the sewer of self-degradation, rampant self-abuse, and unmitigated pustules of indecency and abomination. Still, to Cabo he must go. It was all part of the great plan, and he would do his share and live in praise and glory knowing he had brought the beast of sinful consumption and moral decay to its knees.

He would conduct his business with Passkey, but stay not a moment longer. He knew from his informants that Passkey was planning a sumptuous reception. Passkey would offer him the sins of the flesh, both male and female. He would have to think this over. What was the expression? "When in Rome, do as the Romans do." Who knew what manner of fatal disease he might bring down upon himself, however, if he consorted with the flesh of the Western people. It would be best, he decided, if he had access to a virgin…a young virgin. He must be guaranteed she was a virgin. Perhaps he should take his personal physician with him.

So, he would meet with Passkey who would temporarily remain their puppet in Cabo San Lucas. The product would be shipped from the Middle East, off loaded onto American port facilities that the Arab world now controlled. The product would then make its way to various other ports in Mexico and the United States via cruise ships, tankers, and other shipping lines.

It was a simple matter of sealing off a large tank on each vessel and loading the product into the contained area. Off loading would simply look like the holding tanks were being pumped out or cleaned. The country would be filled with narcotics, everything from cocaine, to heroin, to the ever popular meth.

There was no end to retailers, so distribution was completely assured. It would be only a matter of years until the country that ruled the world would not even be able to rule itself due to the "unruly" growing population of addicts who would help bankrupt and corrode the moral fabric of the society and the entire governmental system. Of course, the system was so corrupt now it needed only a slight shove to go down. It was a slow, but certain death. In the interim, thousands of his fellow countrymen would be illegally crossing the borders from Mexico into the United States. It was not difficult to disguise oneself as a Mexican...just dress in rags and look desperate. The very people who so many Americans had been violating, cheating and using would readily join with the new conquerors. Unfortunately, he could not get his leaders to understand that there would still be a sizeable population not using the drugs who would fight to the finish. His leaders only saw the Americans who frequented bars and clubs, shot and maimed each other randomly, and gave birth to disabled and addicted babies because of their lack of character. He knew there was a huge population that would wage a guerrilla war, just as the early Americans had against the British.

He had attended the best American schools and understood the definite line of demarcation in the society. It was not a line separated by class or wealth. It was a moral demarcation, and it was there, crossing through all socio-economic groups.

But all of that would be years down the road. He would not worry over what might be. Perhaps his uncle would be right, and the remaining population would welcome the law and order that the Muslim world would provide.

For now, he had to make the final Mexican arrangements. He hoped then he would be allowed to drop his alias and return to his country and the beauteous, hot, blessed deserts.

He turned from the window and looked about his sumptuous penthouse. His job did have its perks. He would have his secretary arrange for his private jet to take him to Cabo. He would never stay with Passkey. Instead, he had an entire floor of the Fiesta Pacifica reserved for him and his small entourage. Maybe he would buy the resort and conduct his business from Mexico. He much preferred the weather. And, he reasoned, as long as he was stuck playing the role of the American Mafioso, he might as well steep himself in the part. Perhaps if he fully understood the Americans' vices he'd be a better opponent. He would be forgiven for his transgressions since he was only doing his job for the glory of Allah.

Chapter Nine

BEN closed the door to his office, telling Dina that he didn't want to be disturbed and to hold all calls. He spent an hour on the file Chloe had given him. Only two names attracted his attention, those of Andrew Scott and Jake Starr. It was easy to account for Scott's whereabouts because of his public appearances and work in the legislature. Starr, however, was trickier. The marshal was also a public figure, but not to the extent that Scott was. In addition, it appeared that Starr spent a great deal of time at his ranch, whereas Scott lived almost full time in Glendale.

Having exhausted Chloe's notes, Ben closed the folder and eyed Stephanie's. Before he looked, he knew he should make certain decisions - painful ones. Was he prepared to risk everything to bring the "Cactus Murderer" to justice? If it was Starr, it might well be the end to his career. As Stephanie had pointed out, no one really wanted the vigilante caught or the murders to end. "No one is above the law," he muttered to himself as he opened the folder.

He half expected to see a name scrawled in red ink across a piece of paper. Instead, there was a partial hospital and lab report on an Elizabeth "Betsy" Brunkee. Puzzled, he scanned the autopsy and toxicology reports which detailed the death of the seventeen-year-old from cocaine. The name Brunkee did not come up on his computer when he accessed the available police information programs. He ran the name through the obituary files and again came up empty-handed. He Googled Brunkee's name, still to no avail. Just the fact that the autopsy and tox reports from the coroner's office weren't in the police files raised red flags for him, but when he found there was no death certificate, he knew Brunkee might well be the key to the killer.

The reports were dated a little over two years ago, right before he'd joined the department. An unusual surge in staff turnover in the coroner's department that year was going to complicate the search for whoever signed the documents.

There was still one place he could look that might render some information. High schools kept records of students for god knows how long, so a public high school would probably still have a record of Betsy Brunkee. How many schools were in the greater Phoenix area? Unless, of course, she attended a private school, or a school out of the area. He didn't want to even think about the possibility that she'd dropped out. Social Security might be a source of information if he could ever get past the red tape. She would have had a social security number assigned at birth – when did they start doing that anyway, he wondered. Questions attacked him. A whole list of "what-ifs" materialized on the tablet before him. What if she weren't even from the Phoenix area? What if Brunkee was an alias? He could definitely use Chloe's assistance in this, but he hesitated to ask her after their last meeting.

He reluctantly dialed her number. "You still speaking to me?"

"Of course not. What do you need?"

"Your offer of help still good?"

"Yeah."

"Can you come to my office? I've got an assignment for you. A big one. I think it's the key to the case." He knew she'd be too curious to stay angry.

"I'll be there in an hour," she responded curtly.

There were only a few other pieces of paper in the file, one a police report with practically every other word blacked out, including the names of the victim and the reporting officer. Even the address where the police had found the girl was blacked out.

"Oh, that's helpful," he muttered to himself again. He couldn't help but wonder where Stephanie had gotten this information. Perhaps she was more at risk than he was.

The remaining papers in the folder were notes, small sheets of paper torn from an officer's pad, sketchy at best. He strongly doubted that their meaning would even be clear anymore to the investigating officer.

Surely there was someone in the department who would remember this case, he mused. Would he be sounding alarms if he started questioning people? Probably. This was obviously a cover-up. A big one. So, who'd been quickly promoted then? Or who'd left unexpectedly? Maybe, he shuddered, the question was, who had suddenly died? There was no way he'd be allowed to access personnel files. He felt stymied and regretted that he hadn't schmoozed more with the guys and joined in their bull sessions.

An idea began to percolate. Maybe he should pay a call on Jake Starr. Or better yet, if there was a Mrs. Starr, perhaps that would be even more informative. How could he find out how long Starr had been married to his current wife?

He googled "Jake Star" and was delighted to find several hits on the internet for the famous Arizona lawman, but nothing of a personal nature came up. All newspaper hits were strictly business, and there were few articles at that. It seemed as though Starr was as private as he himself tended to be, avoiding social engagements and fundraisers, preferring to live in relative isolation on his spread outside of Ajo.

To Ajo he would go. He couldn't rightly say what made Starr stick in his craw, but it did, and that was that. Besides, it was the only lead he had...the only one he'd had in the many months he'd been on the case. He'd even call on him in his office. That wouldn't seem unusual; after all, they were both lawmen, and Starr was on the Cactus Murder Task Force. That would give Ben a chance to look around, get a feel for the man, maybe even pump the office staff for information.

He'd assign the high school part of the investigation to Chloe. She was meticulous at that sort of thing. He'd seek out Starr. He had nothing better, and no one else. "Who are you Betsy Brunkee?" he asked aloud.

He had a week until Thanksgiving to work on the case. He pretended that he was still undecided, but deep down he knew he'd go to Cabo San Lucas to spend the holiday with Jere and Stephanie. It would also give him a chance to check on Juana Salcedo. Last year, when it had been his week for the time share, Juana had arranged to clean Ben's suite and had left flowers and special treats for Jere. She'd even smiled at them when they returned to the room once when she was there cleaning.

He'd accumulated a backlog of compensation days, so staying the entire week was not out of the question. The real issue was transportation. He'd checked and found that the airlines were booked and had been for weeks, leaving him no choice but to take the V-Rod or drive his well-worn Chevy pickup. Neither appealed to him, but he decided after a moment that he'd take the V-Rod. He'd done the trip before, so he knew the ins and outs of the journey. The long stretches between fueling stops going from El Rosario across were his only concern. He'd have to carry two small gas cans and hope he didn't have a head wind.

Meanwhile, he'd proceed with the Starr investigation. Glancing at his watch, he decided to postpone his visit to Ajo until the following day. That would leave him time to confer with Chloe. She would also have ideas, and since she worked part-time for a private investigator, she might have resources at her disposal that he didn't have. He buzzed Dina to have her reserve him a department car, preferably a jeep, for his trip the next day. "In fact, make certain it's a jeep," he said emphatically. "I'll be going off road again."

Feeling more upbeat than he had in days, he settled back in his chair with more old obituary reports and waited for Chloe to arrive. Stephanie was right. The key to the case was in the folder. He intuitively knew that the murders were the acts of revenge – undoubtedly revenge for the wrongful death of Betsy Brunkee. How would Starr be related to Brunkee though? She would have been too young to be his girlfriend. If she were his daughter, why would the last name be different? He realized the stupidity of the question even as he asked it. It was not unheard of for the immediate families of police officers to use different last names than their spouses'. Some felt it was good protection against criminals who might want to exact revenge for their arrests and incarcerations.

Could Brunkee have been his wife's daughter from a previous marriage? Was she a niece? Cousin? He hated to admit that there was a very real possibility that the young girl was no relation at all, and maybe he was on a wild goose chase. Maybe he should look at Andrew Scott closer.

Stephanie had said that she'd been told that "the folder might help Ben with the cactus murders." So, the answer was in the file folder. Did she know? If she knew, why hadn't she just told him instead of playing this game? He reached for the phone to call her but thought better of it. No. He would figure it out. She shouldn't have to hand him the murderer on a silver platter, but maybe it was time he had a long talk with his ex-wife and remind her of the law that she practiced.

The more he pondered things, the more his almost happy mood disintegrated. By the time Chloe arrived, he was irritated and snappish. He saw Dina's eyes bulge as Chloe walked confidently past her desk and entered Ben's office. The last time she'd seen Chloe around, Chloe'd been walking quickly the opposite direction.

"Detective Thomas," she said as she breezed through the door.

"Come in and shut the door," he snapped. Not in a mood for silly pleasantries, he quickly launched into her assignment, avoiding any reference to Jake Starr and Stephanie. "Need I say, leave no memorandums about. Be very circumspect. Low key."

"Can I check property records to see what property any Brunkees might own or have owned?"

"I don't think the parental name was Brunkee," he said thoughtfully. Why hadn't he thought about checking out county property records?

Chloe added, "It might help narrow down the number of schools I'd have to investigate."

"Good thinking, Chloe. I don't know though. If this person is well known, he or she might be contacted and forewarned by some well meaning civil servant."

"True. But I doubt that would happen, Ben. How long do people stay at those kinds of jobs?"

"If it's a governmental job of any kind, they seldom leave. Benefits are too good."

"Okay. But there's got to be some way of narrowing the field. This could take two weeks. Maybe more if people aren't cooperative."

"You're right, but I can't take a chance. Good idea, but it won't work. Just check out schools, private and public."

"Should I get an attorney to obtain a court order? A lot of times school records are sealed or private."

He hadn't thought of that either. "Well, we're not asking for information other than confirmation whether the girl attended the school. And we really have no justification for a court order. Just flash your badge and try to look official. If you get lucky and hit the target, get her last known address of record. Say you want to contact the parents or something. Just make something up." He was getting jumpy. Chloe always wanted to go by the book, which was what had made her an excellent cop, on the one hand, but also what had prevented her from really excelling in the field of investigation. It's not that he bent the rules, but there were times when he didn't always play by them. He could see that Chloe was a touch uneasy.

"Okay," she said at last, reluctantly.

"This girl – her death – may be the key to the cactus murders, Chloe. Think about all those young men who have died. We can stop it. I just have to make a connection."

"Okay," she answered again, this time sounding more confident.

"See what you can do in the next two weeks. If you get anything, anything at all, call me, day or night."

"Ben, next week is Thanksgiving. Schools will be closed at least part of the week."

"Yeah. You're right. Shoot. The week after. I'll be out of town, by the way, so you'll have to reach me on my cell. Or you can call me at the Fiesta Pacifica in Cabo. I'll have Dina get the number for you."

"Fine." Iciness invaded her already reserved demeanor. "Anything else?"

The change in her tone was not lost on him. He'd forgotten that she knew about the time-share arrangement with Stephanie at Thanksgiving. He sighed. The hell with it, he thought. If she can go to Papeete, I can go to Cabo. He shook his head, disgruntled that he was being pulled into a woman-thing.

"Thanks," he responded flatly as she stood and hastily left the room.

Chapter Ten

THE trip to Ajo went quickly once Ben escaped the slow crawl on the I-10. He'd hoped to avoid the snarl by leaving after the morning rush hour, but traffic still stalled and slowed. He flipped through radio stations and finally turned it off. His neck and shoulders stiffened. He needed to relax, and now was a good time to practice the new-fangled breathing exercises Stephanie had encouraged him to try. How did it go? Breathe deeply through the nose to the count of four. Breathe slowly out through the mouth to the count of seven. Feeling ridiculous, he shook his head in disbelief, yet he continued the exercise. Within a minute he noticed the tension leaving.

It was a beautiful day, and he clenched his jaw, determined to enjoy it. "Relax," he coached himself. "Breathe. Release."

When had he become so tense? He ran his fingers through his thinning hair and sighed. Was it the job? Was it just him? When had he last laughed? Now that was a discouraging question, especially when he realized he couldn't remember. Start with something simple. When had he last smiled? Got it. He'd last smiled a few days ago with Stephanie. Just a brief, quickie smile though. I just need a vacation, he silently counseled himself. I'll be better after Thanksgiving in Mexico. And he clung to that hope, even though he doubted very much that a week in Cabo would revive him.

Finally, he exited the I-10 and headed into Starr's neck of the woods. He had a vague idea where Starr lived, but topped the jeep off at a station along the freeway exit, just in case driving deserted desert roads took longer than he planned.

He got lucky and found the large ranch on the first foray into the desert. A sign and a cattle guard announced that he'd just entered private property, and he finally realized just how large a spread Starr owned when he drove for twenty minutes before coming upon the ranch house.

The house was long, and low. It was not ostentatious appearing from the outside, yet it gave a hint of aristocracy. He sensed the interior would be sumptuous. The house had been added on to during the years, but most impressive were the grounds filled with courtyards, pools, scarlet and purple bougainvillea, cacti of every variety, and large, old growth varieties of palms, Aleppo, and other flowing shade trees. It was inviting and soothing, and he suddenly felt sleepy and relaxed.

Before he could emerge from the car, two large Doberman Pinschers took position, their stance and bared teeth daring him to go farther. Almost simultaneously, he heard a low whistle, and both dogs took their ease and ran back to the shade of a tall Sumac. As Ben opened the car door, Jake Starr ambled forth from the cool environs of the front veranda.

"Detective Thomas, to what do I owe this pleasure?" Starr smiled, his blue eyes crinkling as he held Ben's hand in a firm and friendly handshake.

Ben liked the man before him, and seeing him in his own environment stirred his sense of camaraderie. Though not overly tall, Starr had a commanding presence. His sun bleached blonde hair, always a bit too long for officialdom, accentuated his azure colored eyes and deep tan. He looked like a strong, rugged man.

There was a cop edge to him that signaled he could be dodgy and treacherous. He seldom spoke, yet others clung to those words. People moved out of his way.

Sizing Starr up in his own environment, Ben questioned why he even suspected him at all. "Just in the neighborhood," he said unconvincingly. "Thought I'd stop by."

"Oh?" It was obvious that Starr didn't believe him.

"Well, I wanted to talk a bit – unofficially."

Starr didn't reply, and Ben felt conspicuous.

"You're on the Cactus Murder Task Force," he tried to sound nonchalant, "and I need some advice – and your opinion on something."

"Come on in."

Ben followed him into the house and saw he'd not been mistaken. The house was immaculate, cool, quiet and extremely opulent. Heavy Mexican woven carpets lay about the deeply oiled mahogany colored floors. The furnishings were massive, leather and manly. Every room that Ben glimpsed into as Jake led him to his office seemed to have a large, rock fireplace.

"Have a seat," Jake offered as the two entered his sanctuary. Ben was immediately mesmerized by the furnishings and décor of the marshal's office. He could tell that it was a room where Starr had what he wanted, where he wanted it. Trophy heads of various animals decorated the walls, along with an extensive arrowhead collection, antique firearms, a shotgun shell re-loader, bows, arrows, an old cavalry saddle, and numerous Indian and Mexican artifacts.

"Quite a room you have here," Ben said in genuine admiration.

"I spend a lot of time in here. Gotta be comfortable where you spend your time. That's my theory."

Ben thought of his own home office. He'd have to do some serious redecorating. Maybe that was his problem. He had no real connection to anything. His personality was not invested in anything but his motorcycle and, he paused, what else did he give a crap about anymore? His boat. Yes. He did love the small sailboat that he'd purchased last summer on a trip to the Oregon coast. A Nor'sea 27. Small enough to trailer, but large enough to carry him around the world if he chose. He felt the boat was his haven, his little nest away from the insanity that he lived in everyday.

"It's fantastic," Ben said in envy, looking about the room."Suits me," Starr answered, watching Ben closely.

"Can I get you something? Iced tea? Beer? Something harder?"

"You know, iced tea would be great. I'm on the clock."

"To hell with the clock. You want a beer?"

"Nah. Iced tea is fine."

Starr spoke in fluent Spanish into a box on his desk, motioning Ben to take a seat. "So," he resumed, enthroning himself into a large swivel desk chair, "what's on your mind?"

Ben stalled a moment, looking about for photos or other memorabilia that would open a doorway to conversation. "Well, Jake, I'm kinda stuck."

"Yeah. You're stuck between and rock and a hard place all right." Ben could feel the lawman studying him closely. "Whatcha got so far? Any real leads?"

"I have a lot of hunches, but as for real leads…"

"So, what's your gut telling you?"

"My gut tells me this is a vigilante, a lone man. My gut tells me it's retribution, probably for the death of someone from a drug overdose. You know, like maybe a daughter, a son, hell, maybe the guy's wife." Ben watched the man across from him for any tell tale signs.

Starr only nodded. Did Ben see him quickly avert his eyes, or was his attention just drawn to the slowly opening door and an older Mexican woman entering, carrying a tray with two frosty glasses and some type of biscuit. Both men remained silent while the housekeeper set the refreshments before them, slightly bowed her head, and noiselessly left the room.

"What else?"

"Well," Ben hesitated. How much should he divulge? "I think people would rather he not be apprehended."

"And you? Would you rather he not be apprehended?"

"I can empathize with the man, but he has no right to kill all those people."

Starr seemed about to say something, but stopped himself. "Well, you know, in my years of wearing a badge, I've learned that sometimes a man's just gotta do what a man's gotta do."

"That can work both ways," Ben commented.

"Yes. It can," he responded, looking Ben directly in the eye, holding his gaze steady. "You got any names? Any possible leads?"

"That's what I wanted to talk with you about, Jake. You're a member of this task force – you and those other people, what are you doing? You got any names? I'm desperate. Either I make a collar or I'm finished."

"I'm afraid, Ben, that you will be finished even if you make a collar – especially if you make the right collar, if you get my drift."

"So I've heard."

"Oh? You got an informant?"

He smiled in response. "If I had an informant, Jake, I wouldn't be here asking for help."

He could tell that Starr didn't fully believe him. "So you drove all the way down here to ask me if I had any names?"

"That and I do spot checks in the area from time to time. I got a guy in Lukeville I talk to regularly. Border stuff."

"Oh, who's that?"

Ben smiled again, but it was a smile that signified he would not be giving a name.

"So, what's going on? The rest of you come up with anyone you can tell me about?"

"No. No, we haven't. To be honest, we've been more concerned with what's going on over the border than on this side," Starr responded.

"So I've heard."

"Ah! You do have an informant!"

"I'm thinking, Jake, that I'm on this wild goose chase to appease Mexican officials. I don't think anyone cares about getting this guy - it just makes us look like good citizens by having me running around the desert following vultures. I'm thinking there's something else, big, going on."

"You're a good thinker, Ben. Be careful."

It was time to change gears. The conversation was becoming inane, and Ben worried about giving too much of Stephanie's information away. "Well," he stretched his legs, looking about. He saw not one picture in the office. "You tell your missus that this iced tea was about the best I ever had," he said as he took a sip.

"I surely will," Jake said, standing. "But it's lemonade."

"No wonder I didn't need to add sugar."

As the two walked to the front door, Ben tried to keep his head from swiveling 360 degrees. "You like living way out like this?"

He could see Starr letting his guard down. "I love it. I love sunrise and sunset the best, but even the heat of the summer is agreeable."

"Your family like it too?"

"It's just my wife and I."

"I'm surprised. Usually women don't like being so isolated."

"My wife had an accident a while back. She fell off a horse and broke her back. She's confined to bed."

"Sorry to hear that," Ben said, genuine feeling in his voice.

"Well, it's one of those nasty tricks that life plays on you."

Ben knew he was pushing his luck. "No kids?"

"No. Like I said, it's just my wife and I."

"Oh. I thought for some reason you had a daughter."

"No."

"Hmm. Must have been someone else."

"Who told you that?"

"Can't really recall right off. But I thought they said you had a daughter, or maybe they said your daughter died? Obviously I have you confused with someone else though. Sorry."

They walked on in silence. Ben was desperate. "You lived in this area long?" he continued as they reached his car.

"Long enough. Lived in this house as a kid. Course it wasn't this big back then."

"Really? That's unusual. You know, to have a family home like this."

"Oh, yeah. My parents and grandparents are buried in the family plot right here on the property. Kind of hard to part with a place when you got family buried on it."

"Yeah. I'm sure it must be. I've never thought about that."

He saw Starr smile a bit sadly.

An idea bloomed in Ben's head. "So, you're saying you have one of those family burial places here? Like in the old days?"

"Yep. Got my place and my wife's place all plotted out too."

"Amazing. I can see why you like it here so much. You've got a lot of history here."

Starr nodded as Ben closed his car door.

"Thanks, Jake. Good to see you."

"Anytime. If I get any leads, or hear anything, you'll be the first to know. Good luck to you. And if you ever want to come on over and work at the U.S. Marshal's office, you just give me a heads up. I can always use a good man," Starr said, sounding sincere.

"Thanks. I might take you up on that,"

Ben watched the man in his rearview mirror watch him drive away. He could hardly contain his excitement. Somehow, some way, he had to get to the family burial plot. If Betsy Brunkee was related to Jake Starr like he thought, he might find her body there.

He'd have to consult someone in county zoning, ordinance, or whatever to ascertain where the plot would be without Starr finding out. How in the hell would he be able to do that? He drove back to Phoenix recalling details and innuendos that he'd filed away for pondering.

"A man's gotta do what a man's gotta do." Now what the hell was that all about? Some wild west philosophical incantation? An excuse? A reason?

And what about the wife? How might he verify Jake's story? Ben chewed anxiously on his cheek as he wondered how he could check out the family burial plot on the property. There were those two damn man-eating dogs. Were they always close to the house, or did they roam? Was the property completely fenced, or was it possible to wander on it "accidentally". Should he get a search warrant? No. Too premature. Questions bombarded him. The answer to everything might simply be in plain sight in the family plot.

He pulled into the parking spot in the garage and took the stairs two at a time to the second floor. Dina handed him three messages from Chloe and one from Stephanie as he entered his office. He wasn't in the mood for talking, though. He needed to think. He needed to access the planning commission in Pima County. Maybe he could get the information on line, or would the county not be computerized? What if the burial area hadn't ever been recorded? This might be a case where he would have to divert Starr away from the property and send Chloe in as some kind of inspector. She'd never go for that. Maybe he could get Stephanie to call a meeting, and then he himself would go as some sort of inspector or county official. Then again, maybe he was completely wrong about Starr. He hoped he was, but if Jake ever found out that he had deceived him in any way, he would have a formidable enemy. It would be over for him. It looked like he might lose no matter what he chose to do.

Chapter Eleven

A week passed, and still Ben didn't have the information he needed. He kept stalling. He hadn't returned Chloe's calls either, and they'd finally stopped. His call to Stephanie had elicited the information that she'd booked him under the name of Benjamin Franklin at the Fiesta Pacifica. It was her little joke always. Ben never used an alias when he traveled, but Stephanie exercised more caution, particularly as she knew that Bill Passkey was somewhere in Cabo. So Ben procrastinated, wanting time away from his conundrum to think things through before he proceeded. Maybe he could con Chloe into checking out the property while he was gone.

He felt like one man against the world. Even his chief had turned apologetic towards him lately, but the man had his own position to protect, so his lamenting of Ben's situation was limited, and guarded. Well, Starr was not going anywhere, and he was. It could wait until he returned from Cabo, along with the autopsy report on another body Immigration had found mummifying in the desert. It was another of Ben's dealers, dead long enough that the body was partially eaten and decomposed. Another drug-runner brought down, maybe by Jake Starr.

He drove Jere to the airport on Friday morning to meet up with Stephanie for their flight. Twenty-four hours later, he headed across Hwy. 60 out of Wickenburg, picked up the 175, then the I-8, hitting San Diego by noon. The Tijuana crossing was tedious as usual, but once past customs, immigration, and the other officialdom of Mexico, he settled into the bike and focused on his southbound journey. He was not so lucky, however, and was pulled over in Ensenada by a cop obviously supplementing his income with *mordida* – bribe money. After arguing with the *policia* as much as he dared, he forked over $50.00 and raced off, swearing under his breath.

The trip down Baja grew relaxing once he got to El Rosario. The highway between the border and El Rosario, however, was a pain in the ass. One small town after another with those annoying little speed bumps seemed to take an eternity. Past El Rosario, traffic thinned dramatically and the weather grew warmer by the mile. The biggest problem, the lack of Pemex stations along the route, forced him to carry two small gallon jugs of gas, something he didn't like to do.

He roared into Mulege later than planned the next evening because he couldn't stand the idea of staying in Santa Rosalia. He'd pressed on despite the dangers of driving in the dark on Mex 1 highway.

Memories of Mulege coaxed a tiny smile from him as he remembered a crazy, romantic week that he and Stephanie had spent in the area on one of their few vacations together. He wondered why they'd not vacationed more. He certainly always had the comp time coming. They'd camped just south of Mulege on Playa el Burro. Their two person tent and a palapa housed them for seven days and nights of total serenity. It was a week of bliss, terminally marred by a ferocious argument the day they left to return to Las Vegas. What had they argued about anyway? His work, probably. He tried to shrug the memory away. That's what they'd always argued about. She didn't get it. He was a cop, not her houseboy, no matter how much money her parents threw at them. There were houses now along that stretch of beach, and he kicked himself in the ass when he thought about his not following through on researching real estate in the area.

The trip from Mulege to Cabo would take a full day, so despite his late arrival, he left at dawn on Monday, watching the sunrise explode over the Sea of Cortez as he flew south, igniting the V-Rod's turbo whenever possible.

He called Stephanie even before he unpacked his small saddlebag.

"Hi, how was the trip?"

"Good."

"You didn't do it in only three days now, did you?"

"No," he lied.

"You little liar."

"Would I lie to you?"

"Okay. You want to meet Jere and me for dinner, or are you too tired?"

"Can we do dinner here? I'm beat, to be honest. But I'd like to have dinner with both of you."

"Perfect. How about 8:00?"

"Good. I'll take a short nap and meet you at the beachside restaurant."

His luxurious room overlooked the beach, and the sound of the surf quickly lulled him to sleep. He hoped the Cactus Murders would fade as quickly as he was fading as he laid his head on the soft, white pillow.

***

Ben's arrival did not go unnoticed. Vincente Basilli approached his limousine as Ben's turbo-charged motorcycle halted in front of the Fiesta Pacifica, despite the valet's frantic arm motions directing him to park elsewhere. Always a fan of the Harley Davidson,

Basilli watched the imposing man dismount and stroll nonchalantly through the front doors of the lobby, still wearing his leathers, brazenly leaving his motorcycle in a "Reserved VIP" spot. He could see that the bike had custom work done on it. He'd have to meet the tall, impressive looking American who dared to drive alone down the long stretch of Baja.

"Get his name," Basilli spoke to his bodyguard. "Find out what room he is staying in. I would like to make the pleasure of his acquaintance."

Some minutes later the bodyguard reappeared. Handing Basilli a note, he spoke in Arabic to his employer. "His name is Benjamin Franklin. Suite 2510. He is alone, but the reservations were made by a Stephanie Thomas, from Phoenix. He has reservations for the week."

"Good, Amhad. We'll meet Mr. Ben Franklin this week," and he chuckled at the name. "These Americans," he said as he pocketed the slip of paper. "Fine. Let us proceed to Villanova's estate and get this business expedited," he directed the chauffeur.

He drummed his fingers lightly on his Moroccan leather briefcase. He wanted to get this meeting over with. He despised Bill Passkey, or Villanova, whatever he wanted to call himself. Clearly his name should be Satan, he mused as the car headed north to Passkey's "Casa Pacifica." What a joke. The house was anything but "pacifica" – peaceful. The man terrorized the help, with his glutinous sexual perversions never satisfied. Basilli promised himself he would not stay for the human desserts that he'd heard Passkey had arranged. It was disgusting, yet remotely tantalizing.

Despite the upcoming meeting, he could not shake Ben Franklin from his mind. There was something about the man that teased him. "Ahmed, I want you to watch for this Ben Franklin.

See who he socializes with. What he drinks, eats, where he visits. When does he arise? Go to bed? With whom does he sleep? Whom does he call? He is a man with a secret, that I can tell you already. He moves with authority and determination, yet his eyes carry the weight of the world."

Basilli watched Ahmed rapidly write down his instructions. Only when Ahmed paused, did he continue. He had employed Ahmed long enough to know that the inflection of his voice was all that was needed to signify his intent. That was his way. Too many words made for confusion, which then caused more needless words. One could drown in words.

"Also, find out about Stephanie Thomas. Who is she? What is her interest in Mr. Benjamin Franklin. Where does she stay? What does she do?"

"It's a good thing to be cautious," Ahmed ventured.

"Ben Franklin is a dangerous man, Ahmed. This is I know. A most interesting, treacherous man." Basilli recalled Ben's posture, his walk, the way he held his head. "He is a man with a lot on his mind. He is perilous, Ahmed. Be careful. Be discreet."

Thirty minutes later the long, overstated limousine pulled up to Passkey's gated, guarded entrance. "I wonder if the security is to keep people out, or in?" Basilli mused.

He heard Ahmed chuckle in deference, wanting only to please. He knew that Ahmed hoped he would get to participate in the evening's activities. Of course, he could never allow Ahmed to participate as an equal, but he might let him help himself to the leftovers.

"Mohammed," Basilli announced as the limo approached the circular drive, "I want you to take Ahmed back to the hotel. Begin your watch on Mr. Franklin immediately, Ahmed," he said turning to the sullen, disappointed bodyguard. "Then return at once and wait for me. I won't be long," he added, glancing again to the chauffeur. "Don't wander off and keep me waiting."

He exited the car to the loud, brassy reception of Bill Passkey, who tried in vain to wrap his arm about Basilli's shoulders.

***

The phone in Ben's suite rang several times before he awoke from his deep sleep. "Christ-o-mighty," he muttered as he looked at his watch. 8:20. He was late, and Stephanie was not a patient woman. "I'll be right there," he said without letting her identify herself.

So much for the shower and shave, Ben mused as he looked at his face and ran a hand over the two day old stubble. His hair stood on end. He looked rumpled. Well, it's not like a date, he consoled himself. It's my ex-wife. Who am I trying to impress?

Another fifteen minutes passed, however, before he exited the elevator and headed for the restaurant, smoothing his hair and raw face, trying to straighten his slightly wrinkled shirt and shorts. He did not notice the Arab face pretending to read the newspaper as he hurried across the large, marble foyer, his flip flops flapping to the beat of his heart.

"Ben, over here," he heard Stephanie's voice and Jere's call of "Daddy," simultaneously. A smile swept over him as Jere raced to take his hand and lead him to the table. It'd only been three days since he'd escorted her to the airport, but he suddenly realized how much he'd missed her.

"Sorry to keep you waiting."

"Don't let it happen again," Stephanie teased. "I mean, we have such a busy schedule this week."

"Okay. I won't be late, if you keep your cell phone off when we're together."

"Deal," she smiled as she turned the buzzing phone off. "You look like hell, by the way. You did drive in three days, didn't you? Never mind, don't answer that. I don't want to know."

He smiled sheepishly and took a sip from her drink.

"Waiter, two Pina Coladas," Stephanie said to the young man who appeared at their table.

"So what have you two been up to since you arrived?"

"The usual. Over-eating, shopping, too much sun."

"Sounds good to me," he said, out of habit giving her his heart-rending little wink. He lowered his eyes instantly. He wasn't here to flirt with her, so why did he do that?

"Daddy, I got a tattoo! Look!"

"Awesome!"

"Mom won't let me get a real one though. A kid in my school has a real one. Mom says I have to wait."

"I say so too."

"You guys are no fair."

They ordered and two hours later finished the gourmet meal. Both moved a short distance to beachside recliners, while Jere played at the surf's edge.

"Damn. I should do this more often," Ben stated, mostly to himself.

"Amen to that," Stephanie agreed.

Neither spoke for some minutes, content to watch Jere play, listen to the lulling sound of the surf, and enjoy the boats bobbing at anchor.

"Did I tell you I bought a boat last summer?" he asked.

"You're kidding me! When did you do that?"

"Remember when Jere and I went to Oregon when I went up for a class reunion?"

"You bought it there?"

"Yeah."

"What did you buy? Are you out of your mind? When are you ever going to use a boat? What kind of boat is it, anyway?"

"Sailboat. And yeah, I'm probably a bit out of my mind." He knew Stephanie had been a sailor before they married. She'd always wanted a small sailboat, but he'd never much heeded her wants, which all seemed like whims at the time.

"So what'd you get?"

They spent an hour discussing his purchase, with Stephanie growing increasingly silent and withdrawn as he waxed on enthusiastically. He could tell she was put out that he'd bought something alone that she had always wanted them to have together. "You'll have to teach me to sail," he added, trying to assuage her hurt. He watched her smile and nod, and wondered himself when in the hell that would ever happen. He could see her steeling herself and trying to look cheerful. It was then that he realized that she had an agenda for this trip, and it would not work for her to become a frump.

"That's wonderful, Ben," she said, trying to sound genuinely supportive.

Should he broach the subject now, or wait and let her wrangle him about until she felt she had him and then came in for the kill. Was this an ex-wife thing? He'd thought things were going smoothly between them, all things considered, but now he wondered if she'd just been playing him. He hated all this second guessing. Women were clever and deceitful, Stephanie more than most.

He'd wait. Let her stew about whatever it was. Why make it easy on her? Maybe it was nothing, after all, but his own growing paranoia.

"Hey, let me get you guys a taxi. I'm going to turn in."

"Can you come for breakfast tomorrow?"

"The buffet?"

"Let's say 10:30?"

"Sure."

He walked them through the lobby to the long stand of waiting taxicabs, a delicious feeling of relaxation taking hold of him.

***

Ahmed watched Stephanie and the little girl, her daughter he presumed, climb into the first taxi in line. He'd learned already that Stephanie Thomas came from a wealthy family, was an attorney, divorced, and had a daughter. He looked to see if Ben Franklin might lean in to give her a kiss on the cheek. He did not, although he kissed the little girl on the top of her head. Interesting. Very interesting.

What interested him even more was the signature at the base of the dinner ticket Ahmed held in his hand. The man had signed as Ben Thomas, not Franklin. A slip of the pen, Ahmed smiled to himself as he pocketed the ticket and gave the waiter a handsome tip.

Chapter Twelve

BY the third day, Ben knew that these few days would never be enough. Every day seemed a fiesta of color and sensation. He ate slowly, savoring each morsel of the flavorful meals set before him. He drank slowly, enjoying equally the sting of the Mexican tequilas and the refreshing cold of his favorite Mexican beers. He moved slowly, as though his entire universe wobbled on its axis. Starting the third day, he slept later, and the hiss of water and pounding of surf outside his open balcony doors lulled him to sleep instead of jarring him awake. For once he was able to leave entirely his job, his stress, his anxiety.

The days melted one into the other, and he relished his routine of breakfasting with Stephanie and Jere at Playa Blanca, then dining with them at the beachside restaurant at Fiesta Pacifica. Each night it seemed the dinner hour stretched longer, and Stephanie lingered later over her Kahlua and cream.

No, he realized, a week was not enough, a month would not be enough. That is when the realization of what he must do slowly and surely began to dawn, leaving him no doubt about his future course of action. He casually set his epiphany aside, however, and continued to loll in the lap of peace.

He lay inert on the beach in the late afternoon sun, watching nothing in particular, yet seeing everything so clearly for the first time since he could not remember. As he lay motionless, he realized he was seeing something that did not make sense. Every afternoon he'd watched a tender travel continuously from cruise ship to shore and back with no passengers aboard. Back and forth, it would disappear for an undetermined stretch behind a breakwater and merchant ship, then it would dutifully return to the cruise liner where it disappeared on the seaward side of the ship. Then, inexplicably it would appear once again on its shore bound journey. It continued in this way for many hours, every afternoon that a cruise ship came to port. Must be loading fuel, he mused, and then dismissed the thought from his mind. Yet it jarred him, and he didn't know why.

Knowing that his afternoon of peace was now perturbed, he sighed and stood, then headed towards the warm, salty water. He'd take one last dip before Stephanie and Jere arrived. In fact, he realized they were a bit overdue now, and he briefly hesitated. That is when he heard his name being shouted.

"Senor Thomas! Senor Thomas!"

At first he didn't recognize the voice frantically calling for him, but when he saw the diminutive figure racing towards him he immediately identified it.

"Juana," he called out. "Over here."

She saw him and instantly veered course. He could see, even at a short distance, her flushed face and perspiration soaked hairline. Fear covered her exquisite features.

He stepped towards her. "Juana, what is it?"

Her heavy breathing kept her from speaking for a moment. "Senor, I am so sorry. I be careful to watch. But they are gone."

Before he asked, he knew the answer. "Who, Juana?"

"Senora Stephanie and the little *nina*. They are gone, Senor Thomas. I so sorry."

"What do you mean gone?"

"They are taken. It is the Bill Passkey from Nogales. I know it is him. I know him. I see him here. I am seeing him this morning at Playa Blanca. I know he has taken them. He came this morning and watched her, and then this afternoon, as I leave, I see her and the little one get into taxi – but it was not taxi – not good taxi. It look like one, but it not taxi. I knew there be trouble." Her speech stumbled over words and phrases.

Ben had read about the taxi scam, and now his wife and daughter had become statistics that the state department would see, but choose to ignore because they saw no faces and had no immediate connection to the victims. Unsuspecting people hailed taxis, only to have the taxi stop after a short distance and thugs get in. Not only did robberies occur, but rapes, beatings, and sometimes even murder happened as the well compensated taxi driver drove down deserted alleys or back roads while unspeakable crimes were perpetrated on the taxi customers. Not just American tourists were targeted. Wealthy Mexicans were also victims of this diabolical assault.

"How long ago, Juana?"

"An hour. It take one hour for me to get here. One hour." He sat her down and waved off the attendants who came to remove her from the "Guests Only" section of the beach.

"Juana," he stopped, suddenly speechless. He asked himself aloud as he looked into Juana's terrified, brown eyes, "What is going on?"

"She think it safe taxi. I have much fear, Senor Thomas," a solitary sob escaping her.

"Do you know where he lives?"

"Yes. I find out when I see him many time ago."

"Where? Where does he live?" Ben could tell an idea suddenly distracted the young woman from her fear.

"Let me go. I get them back, Senor. He trade them for me."

"I don't think so. There's a lot at stake in this. Come, go with me to call the police. My Spanish isn't so good. I need your help."

"The police no do nothing, Senor. Everybody has much fear of Bill Passkey. He is big man in Cabo. In Baja. He is big drug man now. He send drugs on ships now. Planes and ships. No one will help for your wife. He kill people all days and no police do nothing." Her English began to waver between bad and worse. She'd obviously rehearsed her earlier speech in the hour she'd spent getting to him, but she was understandable, and her terror spoke volumes.

"I can't let you go to him. You tell me *now* where he lives. I'll take care of this!" He resisted the urge to violently shake her as she slowly shook her head no. "I can find out elsewhere, if you don't tell me," he threatened. He knew he could easily locate Passkey if he pressed green into any official's hand. She had lost her power momentarily.

"Okay," she acquiesced. "We go. I take you. I meet you here, in lobby, no, by gate at street, at 7:00 this night."

"Why the hell we gotta wait 'till 7:00?"

"Trust me. It best time to get in house and get them. He eat big dinner and drink at 8:00 every night. No missing a night. Even if no persons there, he eat in big room alone. Take one, two hour for to eat."

"How do you know all this?"

"I know because my life depend for me to know."

Ben glanced at his watch. He had three hours until 7 p.m. That would give him time to search Playa Blanca and several of Stephanie's favorite afternoon shops. His racing heart and slick palms welcomed him back to his world, the world he had only minutes ago relished escaping.

***

Vincente Basilli watched the drama unfold on the beach below his penthouse. He saw power literally surge into Ben as he arose from kneeling before the woman in maid's clothing. Was she his paramour? Vincente wondered. No. He didn't think so. So why had she come and sounded an alarm, for Bassili could tell that was exactly the result of her words. He wondered if that meant the stupid ass Passkey had done what everyone had advised him, no, warned him, not to do. Had he taken the woman and the girl? What an idiot.

He could hear Hiro Matsuya inside the suite gathering his papers and other belongings. A most productive meeting, he mused. A Pacific Rim connection would be invaluable. Suddenly the shipping magnate stood beside him.

"A beautiful view," Matsuya blandly offered.

"Yes. I'm thinking of buying this resort."

"A wise idea, especially for business reasons for the next few years."

Basilli smiled in response. "My thoughts exactly." Was Matsuya studying Ben?

"I will take my leave now, Mr. Basilli. Please give my regards to your most esteemed uncle. It is a pleasure to do business with you. Please, stay. Enjoy your view. I can see myself out."

Basilli knew the proper thing to do would be to object and to walk Matsuya to his waiting vehicle, but he didn't want to miss the excitement unfolding below. This could prove to be quite entertaining. He'd been at Passkey's house when Ahmed had called to tell him of the identity of the fictitious Ben Franklin. Basilli, puzzled by the careless use of a pseudonym, sat for some moments pondering the new information.

"Trouble, my friend?" Passkey solicitously asked.

"Hmm. No. Just a little mystery."

"I love mysteries. Care to share?"

Annoyed, Basilli started to brush Passkey off but changed his mind. What the hell. It was no big deal. "Do you know, or have you heard of, anyone named Ben Thomas?"

Both Passkey and Lorenzo exchanged sharp glances. "Why do you ask?"

"Well, I just found out that he is using the name of Ben Franklin. I always wonder about men who change their names for any purpose. Either they are hiding much, or hunting much." Here Basilli paused. "But, I see by your expression that this man is no stranger to you?"

"Let's just say that when I see that bastard dead I will finally have a good day."

"Really? I must hear about this."

Passkey omitted no gory detail of the calamitous story that unfolded in Juneau involving the shipping magnate Matsuya, Chloe Littlebird, Ben Thomas, Juneau's murdered D.A. and a host of the other actors in the massive drug trade drama.

"My my," was Basilli's only response. He instantly saw, or hoped, that perhaps Thomas was in Cabo to take care of Passkey, thus the false name, which would save himself the trouble of probably having to dispose of this most disagreeable man before him.

Basilli watched Passkey work himself into a torturous rage as the man paced the floor, cursing and throwing various items. It was quite a display of low class bad temper as far as he was concerned. He studied Passkey closely as he told Passkey of Stephanie Thomas' presence, and he could see evil begin to broil. He knew then that if the Phoenix detective did not kill Passkey, he would have to, if for no other reason than to rid the world of the most obscene man he had ever encountered.

"I need to ravage someone. I need to kill someone. Tonight!" Passkey screamed.

"Help yourself, my friend," Lorenzo responded, "but you know the rules."

"The hell with the rules! I want that woman and her kid. I'll murder them both."

"Bill, I have warned you before. Your appetites are tolerated here, but under no circumstances will the authorities allow an attack on American tourists. They are off limits!" Lorenzo firmly and loudly asserted already well-established facts.

"You know the cops here hassle tourists all the time." Spit flew from Passkey.

"Only the young, and only the pot-smoking, coke snorting, over-drinking, college kids."

"Yeah, yeah! You hassle the old men and women in their damn Winnebagos and you know it."

"That is nothing. What you plan is something. NO! This will not happen, Bill. Put it from your mind. Choose among the unfortunate Mexicans at your disposal. Leave the Americans alone! What you do on American soil is your business. What you do here is mine!" Lorenzo rose, and Basilli watched Lorenzo's silent, almost invisible bodyguard shift forward, his right arm moving to his inside jacket pocket.

Quickly Passkey smiled. "Of course. I forget myself. I am, after all, a guest in the great nation of Inequality and Corruption. Thank you for setting me straight."

"You think corruption, my friend? I can show you a dear neighbor to the north that gave the word its meaning."

"Gentlemen," Basilli broke in, "please. Let us not ruin the evening with upmanships," as he witnessed darts of daring and hatred ricochet between the two men.

"No to the Americans," Lorenzo whispered in a hiss. "Do you understand?"

Passkey shook his head and forced a smile at Basilli. "I have an appetite for something more entertaining than just fornicating tonight, Vincente. I hope you have the stomach for it."

"I think I do not," Lorenzo spoke first while Basilli wondered if he indeed had the nerve for Passkey's carnal, savage indulgences he had heard so much about.

"Regrettably, my friend, I too must pass on your sumptuous desserts," Basilli unexpectedly found himself saying. "I must make the last arrangements for the ports of call to begin unloading and transporting your merchandise. Perhaps another time?" he said politely as he arose, looking about for his jacket. He could see that Passkey knew he was being insulted by his turning down the luscious, lascivious looking girls Passkey had paraded before them during dinner.

"Save room for dessert, men!" Passkey had laughed, as the girls, some appearing to be terrified, had tried to seductively pass through the room.

"Of course. I understand," the host angrily responded. It was obvious to Basilli that Passkey did not understand at all how grown men could resist the urge to inflict pain and humiliation on the weak prone before them.

"Some other time. Perhaps before you leave Cabo, then?" he asked, looking directly at Basilli.

"Yes. Perhaps. That would be fine."

As though perfectly timed, Ahmed arrived in the limousine as Basilli left the house with Lorenzo, saving him from having to return to the city with Lorenzo, knowing Lorenzo would talk more than he should, and fearing Lorenzo would say more than he would later be comfortable with.

"I apologize for my associate," Lorenzo said as he walked Basilli to the car. "It's unfortunate that he has this side to him. It will be his downfall. Of this I have no doubt."

"Yes." Basilli nodded.

"I hope for his sake he does not touch the American woman."

"The Americans are more special than your own women?" Basilli's voice was heavy with condescension, which he knew would not be lost on the man.

"My people are expendable for now, but it is for the greater good of Mexico. There will be a day when a Mexican flag will wave at the White House in Washington, D.C. My people now are only martyrs to a cause long in coming, but coming all the same. It is working, my friend. Soon. The border, the drugs. It is all part of the plan. It is our own Manifest Destiny."

Basilli nodded, the full impact of what Lorenzo was telling him beginning almost to stagger him. It all began to fit. And he, Basilli, was now part of the plan that would bring the world's giant to its knees, and in its death throes it would be begging for mercy in Spanish. The American media estimated there were 12,000,000 illegal immigrants in the country, but Lorenzo tonight had revealed that the number was, in fact, more than six times that amount. Between five and ten thousand crossed the border illegally every single day. The Americans were crippled by their own laziness and self-indulgence. They were, according to Lorenzo, entering the final throes now.

It had been a night Vincente Basilli would not forget. It would be a night he hoped to recount as he'd sit in the desert sand of home, his wise uncle nodding approval and vilifying the lazy, hedonistic, evil America. The information was crucial, however, for he now realized his people would have to take down the Mexicans also, and they were a tenacious, feisty, determined group. But, for now, he was stuck in Cabo San Lucas, finalizing arrangements for the offloading of cocaine and meth from merchant ships to cruise ships. It was, as the Americans were wont to say, a piece of cake. He himself had dreamed up the scheme, and it was working most excellently.

The drugs were pumped into containers in the bilges of the tenders, then ferried to a cruise liner where they were pumped into a septic holding tank that had been closed off and lined with heavy plastic. Then, when the cruise ship came to Los Angeles or its port of destination, the drugs were pumped off, as though they were sewage, into boats that casually went about their business unloading pure cocaine, meth, heroin, opium, whatever was on the menu, instead of sewage. It was beautiful, and it would work for some time, although he could see problems down the road, but that would be months away - maybe years.

Passkey had made similar arrangements at the airport, and at least one flight a day had a drug pumped into a holding tank. Poor passengers invariably had to wait in long lines to use the toilets aboard the planes. It seemed there was always one nowadays that was out of order. The beauty of the Mexico flights was that people seldom flew them every day. They were vacation flights, so therefore no one would get suspicious of a continuously out of service toilet. Basilli laughed. They didn't call drugs "shit" for no reason.

***

The Harley roared to life as Ben sped the short distance between the two resorts. A careful check at Playa Blanca by the management revealed that Stephanie and Jere were indeed not present. Nor could Ben espy them as he rode slowly through the crowded streets of Cabo, looking intently into the small shops. Holding onto the last straw of hope, he returned to his hotel, but the two were not waiting at the beachside restaurant as they had been every evening.

He had to do something. He couldn't wait until 7:00. His mind and his stomach churned in anxiety. Finally, he knew he could no longer hesitate. He picked up the phone in his room and placed the only two calls he knew would do any good. He called Chloe who promised to be on the next flight. And then he called him – Jake Starr. "Jake, I need help," he choked, and then a torrent of words flowed.

Chapter Thirteen

A sudden gasp erupted as Chloe Littlebird's head snapped back as she was abruptly lifted from her squatting position. Head on fire, she fell heavily on her back, wincing in pain as her former injury screamed in agony. Grabbed by her neck and coat front, she was picked up and violently thrown again.

Fiery, sharp stabbing pains ran rampant through the scar tissue that covered her right scapula. Her spine seared with a white hot streak and went numb. Blood seeped into her mouth from her jaws slamming together, loosening back teeth. Her throat, paralyzed from the iron grip that had almost crushed her windpipe, struggled to gasp air. Every ounce of her 120 pound frame pleaded to fight back, and she rolled to her knees, desperate to suck in air but only able to draw a tiny stream of oxygen, not enough to sustain any effort. Defeated, she crumbled back to earth as her attacker strode purposefully towards her, stopping short of sending his foot into the side of her head. She closed her eyes, preparing to die. *Oh Mack*, she thought, *I love you so*. She pictured her absent lover waiting for her in Tahiti. She worried that he'd never know why she didn't show up.

Her attacker unexpectedly stopped, bent over, and peered into her face. "What the hell are you doing here?"

Despite her effort to answer, only sobs came as she slowly shook her head and rolled to her back. Sky blue eyes peered down at her. She tried to answer as she choked on her sobs, still struggling to suck in air.

He laid her on her back, stretching her arms flat on the ground above her head.

She sensed she was safe, that he would not attack again. She saw concern crowd his expression. He began speaking to her in a low voice, and she had to stifle her gasps to hear him.

"Slow your breathing. Stop gasping. It'll come back." He squatted beside her, running his hand through his hair. "What the hell are you doing here?" he asked again.

She noticed more oxygen was creeping down her windpipe. Her hammering heart slowed, but she still fought for oxygen. Tears flowed down the sides of her head. At that moment she hated Benjamin Thomas.

Within minutes her breathing returned to normal and her trembling stopped. She tensed as her attacker gently raised her to a sitting position. "You need some ice. Can you walk?"

"I think so," she cautiously whispered, fearful of talking lest her throat constrict again.

"Never mind. I'll carry you."

Before she could protest, Jake Starr swooped her up as though she weighed nothing. As she looked into his eyes, she could see disbelief and rancor mix.

"You got some explaining to do, young lady."

"I can't talk," she whispered again.

"You'll be fine. That's a powerful hold I just put on you, but there's usually no damage…if you're lucky."

***

Surreptitiously she tried to study Jake Starr who looked deep in thought as he swiveled back and forth in his chair, his feet propped on his desk. She half sat, half reclined, before him after her life-threatening escapade in his family's private burial plot.

She watched as he took off his hat, scratched his sun bleached head and sat upright, bringing his feet to the floor.

"Let's try this one more time, Miss Littlebird."

"That was Ben on the phone, wasn't it?" Chloe demanded, more than asked.

"Yes, that was your cohort in crime, Ben."

"No, Marshal Starr. We…I have not committed a crime."

"Well, how about trespassing for starters?"

"What a load of bullshit! How about me being a victim here?" The exclamation flew from her before she could stop it. Her throat ached in response.

"Miss Littlebird, may I remind you that you are speaking to a U.S. Marshal? May I remind you that you have been apprehended on property that is clearly marked as private and no trespassing allowed? May I remind you that I could have you arrested for grave robbing even?"

"This is ridiculous."

"May I call you Chloe?"

She nodded affirmatively.

"Chloe, our mutual friend has a problem. Let's turn our attention to that for now and deal with your and Ben's transgressions later."

Again she nodded in reply. "Do you believe me now that it was Ben who called me on my cell a few minutes ago?"

"Yes, ma'am I do. He confirmed the call no less when he spoke with me. Despite my anger at this intrusion obviously drummed up by my well-meaning, but misguided friend, I am deeply concerned about what Ben may do if we don't act quickly. My power cannot get him out of a Mexican prison, and that's where he's going to land if we don't take immediate action."

"I know. I'll call the airlines and get on the first flight. I..." Before she could finish he interrupted.

"That'll never work. We need to leave now. I think I can get access to a private flight. We'll be airborne in forty-five minutes and in Cabo in less than two hours. You won't have time to go home and pack – if you choose to go with me, at any rate."

"I can go as is," Chloe said, feeling a wave of relief, followed quickly by a stab of suspicion. Maybe this would be Starr's way of getting rid of two problems at once, she mused. He could easily be in collusion with the Mexican police to put both her and Ben away, or maybe he even had ties with the Mexican drug lords. Her overactive imagination, stimulated by her recent misadventure, flung terrifying visions through her head as she pictured Starr throwing her from the plane, turning Ben over to the Mexican mafia to be tortured and executed, selling Jere off into white slavery, and...

As if reading her mind, she saw a smile tickle his lips.

"I know what you're thinking. Don't worry, you're safe with me."

"I'm trusting you, Starr, only because Ben needs my help. I wouldn't step foot out that door with you otherwise."

"If that's how you feel, you're taking a big gamble there."

"That's how I feel."

"You must care for him very much."

"I do." She paused, then added, "He saved me."

"Well, you can tell me that story some other day. Come on, let's go."

She stood, showing more confidence than she felt, and followed him to his car as he talked on his cell phone, making arrangements for a plane and pilot. "There's a little known landing strip outside Lukeville. Our ride will pick us up there."

She had never felt more vulnerable in her life, but she found herself following Starr despite her having every reason not to. As Ben had suspected, she'd found Betsy Brunkee's gravesite in the family plot. She'd been busy photographing it when Starr came upon her. He'd viciously attacked her, kicking her camera away, a look of venomous hatred in his eyes.

Once he finally recognized her, he carried her to his house and had seen to it that she was administered to. *Probably his stable hand*, she thought as the old Mexican called to aid her expertly tended to her injuries. She'd been no match for Starr. Besides the fact that she was on the wrong side of the law in this little caper, she sensed that she'd also violated the man's privacy and threatened him on an emotional level. When he first began to speak, his words terse, his anger apparent, she tried not to recoil in fear.

"What the hell are you doing on my property?"

"I want to know who Betsy Brunkee is," she'd said as defiantly as she dared.

"What the hell business is that of yours?"

She stopped, not sure how much to reveal.

"Who sent you on this outing?"

She vowed she would not give Ben away.

"Never mind. I know. Benjamin Thomas. And what has planted a bug up his ass about my deceased step-daughter?"

"So she is your step-daughter, then?" Chloe ventured.

Starr only stared at her. She saw contempt written on his face.

Boldly, she blurted, "And where is her mother? Is she mysteriously buried here too?" She almost cringed at her audacity.

There was no immediate response. Then, "My wife is bed-ridden due to a broken neck. Would you care to photograph her also?" his disdain clearly evident.

"I…" Chloe was trying to process this new information. She sat speechless, until her cell phone rang, and the fateful call from Ben intervened in her interrogation. Not wanting to sound an alarm to Ben – his problems were worse than hers - she listened, watching Starr watch her, and then told Ben she'd be there on the next flight.

She could tell Starr hadn't totally believed her until his own phone rang a few minutes later. She watched him as he listened to Ben, and she saw alarm replace disgust. There was no doubt in her mind that Starr, for whatever reason, would help Ben. She didn't understand it. He should have been rejoicing that Ben was neck deep in shit – or could it be that Starr was reacting to the news of Stephanie Thomas being held captive? Chloe wondered if she were connecting dots that really existed – or were they just a figment of her imagination. How would Starr know Stephanie? Of course, the task force. Would he be attracted to her? Of course. She was beautiful, intelligent, tall, willowy and elegant. Chloe'd seen men look at her as she'd walked through the courthouse. But maybe that was not the connection, maybe it was the fact that Ben, a fellow law enforcement officer, was in trouble.

She held on as Starr drove with alarming speed, and after twenty minutes they arrived at a one-runway, no-name airport about ten minutes from the border crossing of Lukeville. Almost simultaneous with their arrival, a small jet approached the runway and landed, leaving only ten yards at the end as buffer zone. She followed Jake as he trotted to the waiting plane.

"Sit down. Buckle up," he directed as she entered the small cabin, and then he pulled the door closed. She'd hoped to talk with him en route, but he disappeared into the pilot's cabin. "Well, at least I won't get thrown out of the plane if he's up there," she said softly, relieved.

***

Ben hung up and lay back on his bed. He was falling apart over this, and he had to get control of himself. Of all the times in his life, he had to hold himself together now, no matter what, or he could jeopardize the safety, even the lives, of his wife and daughter. Wife. No, ex-wife. It didn't matter. He still loved her. He could see that so clearly this week. Had he ever stopped loving her? He was an idiot at love, and an expert at not showing his feelings. Perhaps that had been their problem. Him. Him and his obsession with a job that was now killing him and everything he cared about. A deep sob started to erupt, but he held it in check. He would get control of himself, here and now. He was no good to Stephanie, Jere or himself in this state. He had the posse coming. He knew Starr was the best – and so was Chloe. They'd be here soon. He knew he couldn't act alone, and he couldn't count on the local police for help.

And Juana…That she would put herself back in harm's way for him and his family brought a lump to his throat. He couldn't let her do this. When she came at 7:00 he would hog tie her if needed, but he'd not allow her to put herself in jeopardy. She'd already suffered too much at the hands of Bill Passkey. Everybody'd suffered too much. Chloe's career was ruined because of the man. He'd cast Juana and her children away as though they were garbage. He left a veritable wake of dead bodies wherever he went. Ben silently vowed he would end it, once and for all. As far as he was concerned, Bill Passkey would not leave Mexico alive.

He got up and went to his saddlebags. Deep in the bottom, concealed in an oiled rag, was his 9mm. There were hundreds of

Americans in Mexican jails for carrying concealed weapons over the border. Most often, people just forgot that they had their .22 or rifle or shotgun, whatever, in the trunk or glove box of their car. It didn't matter. The Mexicans sent them to jail for even having bullets lying around. And you didn't get out of Mexican jails – he knew that. No mercy. It made his blood boil. Supposedly Mexican officials didn't want guns brought into the country, thinking they would be sold to Mexicans. How ridiculous, he silently scoffed. The Mexicans all had guns – who were they kidding? He'd heard countless stories of people robbed at gunpoint while vacationing south of the border.

He'd hesitated about bringing the gun, but some foreboding had over-ridden his good judgment, and now he was thankful that he'd brought it along with two loaded clips. He knew Starr would come armed, but Chloe wouldn't be able to get on a plane in the states with a gun – unless it was in her luggage, and the odds of it being ex-rayed and detected made getting it through not favorable. Then there'd be Mexican customs – always a hit-and-miss proposition. No, Chloe probably wouldn't have a weapon. Maybe Starr would bring extra. Ben realized he should've asked him about that.

He thought back to his call. He didn't feel shame or remorse for his breakdown on the phone, and he instinctively knew Starr would never hold it against him or think the less of him. There was something about the man that seemed protective. Understanding. Empathetic. Ben, who'd grown increasingly wary and suspicious over the years, intuitively trusted Starr, which was making his investigation into the man more and more difficult. Is that why he hadn't returned Chloe's calls the week she was sleuthing for him, searching for the mysterious Betsy Brunkee? Why did Ben give a shit if Mexicans carrying drugs were dying out in the desert anyway? Why should he care, really, especially given his current circumstances? And did he really have any evidence it was Starr? So far all he had was that Starr owned a ranch out in the boondocks where some, *some* – not all, of the bodies had been found. Plus, Starr was somehow connected to a Betsy Brunkee, which might have no bearing on anything.

He shook his head. He wasn't thinking clearly or logically. In reality the fact was he had, at best, only mildly circumstantial evidence against Starr. What did Betsy Brunkee have to do with it? Granted there was a mysterious cover-up over her death, but that in no way indicated Starr was involved, or even knew the woman. At the back of his mind, an idea was trying to enter, but he was too preoccupied with his own plight to spend more time thinking about Starr's possible guilt. How could he think that of the man who was now en route to save his ass? He couldn't.

Glancing anxiously at the clock, he was dismayed to see only half an hour had crawled by since he'd talked with the posse. It seemed an eternity. He noticed, however, that he had more control of himself. He could do this. He needed to steel himself for the action of his life. Passkey would go down. Ben had to be smart about this – not emotional. He had to be hard, ready to shed the blood of innocent people if unfortunately necessary – whatever it took to get Stephanie and Jere back. He refused to think about the indignities that Passkey might do to them. He shook his head violently, and his resolve hardened.

The more he thought about Passkey, the more determined he became. The whole Juneau escapade three years earlier rushed back. That'd been the crime spree of the century for the Alaska capital, and Passkey had directly and indirectly been the cause of most of it. How the man had escaped still baffled him. People like Passkey deserved a death far worse than they ever got.

He left his room a different person than he'd entered. He left it a man of determination and resolve. A man with no conscience. A man with no fear. A man who carried death with him.

Chapter Fourteen

CHLOE settled into her seat and what seemed only moments later saw the brilliant blue of the Sea of Cortez appear out her window. Something about the sea, sand, and sun, stretching endlessly mesmerized her. How she longed to live along a deserted shore, arising every morning with the brilliant red sun bursting over the horizon, sleeping with the gentle sound of the sea lapping in her front yard. Baja enthralled her. The people, the food, the beauty of the long, slender stretch of land. It was, technically, the first foreign country she'd ever been to, if she didn't count Canada, which she'd crossed into on some of her forays up the Stikine River in Alaska when she'd worked for the Alaska State Fish and Game Division.

She clearly remembered her first trip to Baja. Ben had driven her to Rocky Point, a favorite Arizona destination, on his motorcycle. She'd been enchanted. It was all so new, so exciting, and for her, so foreign. After three years in Phoenix, however, she could see that Arizona was slowly evolving into another Mexican state. The change was rapid and scary. Well, she'd gladly move to a small Mexican beach town if the Mexicans wanted to trade places, but she knew the immigration issue was far more complicated and serious than just swapping countries. She'd spent a lot of time in some of the border towns doing investigative work of one kind or another, and what she'd seen horrified her. Often hundreds of Mexicans at a time crossed the border, despite the border patrol's efforts to stem their passage. The border bled a steady stream of desperation. She knew there had to be far more than twelve million illegal aliens in the states.

And she knew, despite the many honest, hard-working, good people who came for jobs and a better way of life, that criminals of the worst sort also crossed over. Ben had once told her that 95% of the crime in Phoenix was committed by illegals. It gave all Hispanics a bad name, unfortunately.

Once she saw the hovels that so many of the people lived in, she completely sympathized with their plight. She would have crossed the border also had she been in their situation. What if Canada, Mexico and the United States just opened their borders for free passage for all North Americans? She wondered if after the first rush of movement, supply and demand would reign, and things would settle quickly.

She thought of Ben and tried to picture what he was doing while he awaited their arrival. He wouldn't be sitting still, that was a certainty. She prayed he wouldn't do anything foolish. Even Jake Starr had limits in Mexico.

What would she do if she saw Bill Passkey? She immediately knew that after she spat on him, she would shoot him in the kneecaps, something where he would suffer for all time, like she suffered because of his Alaska caper. Suddenly she realized she was gritting her teeth, squinting, and clenching her hands.

She closed her eyes, willing thoughts of Bill Passkey to die. She needed to think about the situation at hand. Jake Starr would have a plan though. He was a man who knew all the right people. He had connections. He was obviously powerful to be able to commandeer a jet at a moment's notice and fly into Mexico unannounced. Was he crooked? If he could save Ben, she didn't even care. In fact, she resolved that once Ben, Stephanie and Jere were safely stateside, she would quit the Brunkee investigation and the cactus murders and leave. Mack needed her – she needed him. She'd wasted enough time coming to her decision; she didn't want to dally any more. She regretted her intrusion into Starr's life.

But she had accomplished her mission. She'd confirmed that Brunkee was Starr's step-daughter who died of an overdose. He covered up her death – probably to save his career. She couldn't blame him, but it didn't seem like something he'd do. Maybe he'd done it for the girl's mother. Still, it seemed out of character. But the media would have crucified him because of his near celebrity position. The governor referred to him as her Wyatt Earp, the best lawman of the century. Yes, he would have been massacred if the media had gotten hold of him. She'd seen it happen before.

***

In his palatial hacienda, Miguel Lorenzo sat on his plush, white leather sofa, feeling the long nails of his lover gently stroke his neck. The ringing of his phone disturbed the evening's ambience. Who the hell would be calling him?

"Yeah," he growled inhospitably.

"Lorenzo, this is Starr," Jake abruptly announced.

He half choked on a mouthful of tequila he'd just bolted. "Jake? You sound like you're in a tunnel."

"No, aboard a private jet, heading your way, in fact."

"To what do I owe this pleasure?" he asked nervously.

"Cut the shit, Lorenzo. We need to talk."

"Anything, Jake. You know I'm here for you." How could Jake have found out about the folder? Would the woman have given it to him instead of the cop on the case?

"I need safe landing at the strip by Todos Santos. No cars. No officials. I need a vehicle though. I'm carrying. I don't need any police interference."

"What's going on, Jake?"

"I'm coming for Ben Thomas and his wife and kid. Your pal Passkey has the wife and girl."

Miguel Lorenzo's voice failed him at hearing the news of Passkey's duplicity and disobedience. He knew it would be a serious matter when he heard Jake Starr on the line, but he thought it would be over the information he'd slipped Stephanie Thomas, information that only three people were privy to, information he knew would bring Jake Starr down if needed, and he felt it was needed. No matter what Passkey said to pacify him, Lorenzo fumed at the deaths of the young drug runners, and he strongly suspected that the deaths were the act of revenge by Jake Starr. He also knew that if Starr ever found out that it was he who had overdosed the girl, he would be dead in a heartbeat. He had helped Starr cover up the death, trying to act like an ally, trying to cement a bond between him and the most powerful lawman in Arizona. News of the girl's death and how she died would have spelled ruin for Starr's career. Lorenzo had planned to take the marshal down by exposing the cover-up. He almost clapped his hands when he heard that Starr's mission seemed to be focused on Passkey.

"Jake, you gotta believe me. I told him no in no uncertain terms. Leave the Americans alone, I told him."

"Just meet me at the runway, Lorenzo. I got business with Passkey first, then we'll talk about the other business later."

Before he could answer, Starr clicked off. Shit! He knew! Could he deny it? Probably pointless, especially with Stephanie Thomas now held captive. It would come up somehow. His whole cover was going to be exposed. He had to decide now – was he going to be a Mexican or an American. He'd played both roles long enough. He had to get off the proverbial fence. He was either Michael or Miguel. Who was it going to be?

"I'll be back later," he barked at his mistress as he snatched his keys from the ornate bowl in the foyer of his elegant Mexican hacienda. He didn't wait for her sulky response to echo through the rooms, but headed hastily to the large SUV at the far end of his five-car garage. How the hell was he going to handle this? Obviously, the game was up. He had not only just revealed that he knew Passkey, but he vehemently berated himself even more for his stupid decision to give the files on Starr's daughter to Stephanie Thomas. He knew the lawyer would pass the file on. It was a no-brainer. But he hadn't expected Starr to discover the betrayal until after his arrest. Starr had cost him thousands upon thousands of dollars by killing the drug-runners though. The runners were his idea, and his bread and butter. Their sales paid for his incidentals – cars, boats, planes. It was his little side business. None of this would have happened had Passkey not convinced the *jefes* that the deaths were of no consequence and a way to keep the Americans occupied. "Look at the BIG picture," Passkey always argued.

Lorenzo peeled out of the garage, leaving the smell of burning rubber in the air. He drove the large Escalade recklessly down his long driveway, not stopping to check traffic before he skidded sideways onto the highway. He chewed nervously on his lower lip. He didn't want to deal with Starr under any circumstance. He could see now that it'd been stupid to turn the folder over to the woman. How had the marshal figured things out so quickly? He'd kill Passkey this very night if he had to – anything to appease the Americans.

Despite the fact that the gringos were showing up illegally, carrying weapons, he knew not to call any officials. He had to move carefully, align himself with the most powerful group. His immediate bosses were in Acapulco. He didn't have time to confer with the head honchos of the cartel. The most powerful for now were the Americans. He would become Michael – for the time being he would align himself with the Americans. They at least wouldn't murder him because of one bad judgment call.

"Answer the damn phone, Passkey," he said aloud as the rings annoyingly continued.

Finally, "Yeah."

"Don't touch that woman and girl. You touch them, you're a dead man."

"What makes you think I have them?"

"Cut the shit, Passkey. You have them. Take them back NOW."

"You know, Lorenzo, you're a small fish in a big pond. You're way out of your league when you're talking to me. I can cut any deal with your *jefes* that I want. I don't need you, and I don't answer to you."

"Passkey, you dumb shit, you have no idea what and who you are up against."

"Screw you, Lorenzo."

He started to reply, but the dial tone abruptly interrupted his vituperative.

He'd deal with Passkey once he calmed Starr down. He'd take Starr to Passkey's if he had to. The cop would be there to. Let them kill Passkey. They could easily flee, and Miguel could feign ignorance. Better yet, maybe he'd leave with them. That might convince them that he was truly on their side. But when 80 million or more Mexicans took to the streets in the United States, Lorenzo would put on his other hat – his sombrero.

He parked and paced along the runway. Had he known they were so far out he would have gone to Passkey's and retrieved the woman and girl himself. He could have been a hero, no questions or doubts.

***

In the pilot's cabin, Jake Starr wasted no time making his other connections.

He'd easily detected the edge in Lorenzo's voice. He knew it had to be Lorenzo who'd given the information to Stephanie Thomas, who Ben had to have gotten it from. So why would Lorenzo turn on him? Unless he'd played him all along? The thought made him straighten as the dawning realization arrived ever so stealthily. It wasn't like him to misjudge so badly.

Lorenzo had worked for him in a NEC, Non-Enforcement Capacity. Basically, he'd been a snitch, ratting out Mexican suppliers and felons, but never really the big guys – always just minor players on the fringe. He realized, too late, that if his hunch was correct, Lorenzo took the position solely to keep tabs on the U.S. Marshal's Office, Immigration, and DEA. Starr had been "encouraged" to hire Lorenzo by a superior in Washington, who'd explained that he was doing a favor for a foreign head of state that the vice-president had taken into his confidence. Starr knew now he should've smelled him a mile away, but he hadn't. It all went back to the cover-up – a bad idea, and he'd known it at the time. He'd had a gut feeling this one would bite him in the ass – and it had. What he'd done was not so much illegal as unethical. From his years in law enforcement, he knew it was not uncommon for public figures to go to great lengths to suppress undesirable information about family members. It was unfortunate that he'd chosen that route.

Should he kill Lorenzo? Threaten him? Use his knowledge to apply leverage to get Lorenzo to rat out his *companeros*?

Starr deplaned first, followed by Chloe who, he was certain, Lorenzo had never seen. Her demeanor would not be lost on Miguel. Even though she was small, the way she carried herself strongly hinted that she was a cop.

He ignored Lorenzo's pro-offered hand. This would be the first of many insults, something he knew the Mexican's pride could not abide.

"Stay here with the plane," he shouted over the dying engines. "We'll be leaving in a few hours."

"I can take you to him," Lorenzo started.

"I know where he lives. I don't need any more of your help, Lorenzo," Starr spat, staring the man down.

"Jake," Lorenzo began, sounding nervous.

He wondered if the weasel before him would apologize. Maybe deny? "Just shut up before you dig your hole deeper," he growled. "Keep the f*ederale*s away from the plane."

"Yes. Yes. Of course."

"How many security men does Passkey have?"

"Only the ones at the gate. Every few hours someone patrols the beachfront, but mostly people try to stay out of his sight. You can approach by the beach the most easily. He dines at 8. He won't be watching."

"I need your piece."

"I don't carry, Jake. It's illegal in Mexico."

"Bullshit. Don't insult me. Just give me your piece, or I'll take it from you."

Sheepishly, Lorenzo handed over his 9mm.

"You got any more clips?"

" In the car. In the glovebox."

Starr handed the gun to Chloe who expertly checked the clip and safety, then secured the gun inside the waistband of her trousers. It was plain that her performance was for Lorenzo's benefit. Between Ben, Chloe, and himself, he almost felt sorry for Lorenzo and Passkey. He watched Lorenzo gnaw on his lips. He knew then that Miguel Lorenzo would align himself with the gun-toting Americans, at least for now, for there was no doubt who would emerge the victor – at least in this round.

Chapter Fifteen

"MOMMY, I'm so scared," a piteous whimper in the darkened room brought Stephanie back to her senses.

"It'll be okay, Jere. Shhh. It'll be okay." She struggled to keep her voice low and calm, not wanting to give the men any reason to come into the room where she and Jere were now held captive, tied at the wrists, back to back.

Her nose hurt where the man had back-handed her when she'd asked him, politely in Spanish, to exit the taxi. Blood had splattered onto the window, and Jere had become hysterical. When the second man grabbed and gagged her daughter, Stephanie lost complete control. The first attacker, the big one, punched her in the face, rendering her senseless. Her swollen eye throbbed, and her cheek ached. She sat disheveled, terrified, and angry. She'd kill the bastards if she ever got the chance. She'd seen them. She'd hunt them down if Ben didn't beat her to it.

Ben. Where was he? How long until he discovered that they were missing? How would he find them? Were they being held for ransom? She'd read State Department reports that ransom demands were the big rage now in the cities. She knew if Americans truly knew all the hazards that existed south of the border, they'd never venture there. She didn't want to think they were being held for some other, sinister purpose.

"Daddy will save us, Jere. Don't cry. Shh. Your daddy will come." Even as she said it, she knew it to be true, and for a brief moment she felt triumphant and elated.

She could hear voices from time to time, otherwise the rustling of the evening breeze in the palm trees lulled her. She knew by the distant sound of surf that they were somewhere along the coast. If they somehow got free, she'd know which direction she'd have to head to get to safety. But what if there were people outside on guard? Still, she worked at twisting her wrists this way, then that, trying to free them from their bondage. Her wrists were raw and bloody, her hands sticky with blood.

"Mommy, I want to go home. Let's not come back here next year," Jere pleaded through small sobs.

"Shhh. We won't, Jere. We'll go to Disneyland, okay? Would you like to go to Disneyland? Or Paris? Paris would be better. We could go to the Louvre. You could learn French." She talked quietly of the future to calm the girl.

Both grew silent, listening to the sounds of the house, shuddering when the booming male voice yelled into the phone that rang. He was far enough away that his words were not distinct, but the tone was, and it was an angry, hateful, vicious tone that made Jere cry and Stephanie struggle to remain in control.

The two captives, blind folded, had been half-carried, half dragged into the villa. They now sat on the floor, wrists bound with thin nylon strapping, the kind used to bind electrical wires. Stephanie's ankles were secured too tightly, and she'd lost feeling in her feet. They had not bound Jere's feet, however.

"So. Who have we here?" A male voice had pompously asked, not really needing an answer. "My my my. You're in a pretty fix, aren't you ladies? You rest awhile. I'll be back. We'll play some games later. Do you like games, little girl?" And the man had laughed the most blood curdling, evil laugh Stephanie had ever heard.

"You leave my daughter alone, you bastard," she hissed.

"Oh my. A feisty one. I like feisty women. I have a game for you too, don't worry." The heinous laugh erupted again as the man departed.

Stephanie somehow stifled a scream. Her baby. If the man hurt her baby she would go insane. Somehow she had to get Jere out. She renewed her efforts at the nylon line. She lost track of time. When would the monster return?

Did she hear a noise in the room? A rat? "Is someone there?" she asked in a small voice, trying to peek from under the blindfold, her heart pounding violently.

"Hush. *Soy yo*. Juana. Must be quiet. Shhh."

Stephanie felt the young woman move to her side and begin sawing on the nylon bonds with what must have been a serrated kitchen or steak knife. Juana spoke to them in a quiet, calming voice. Stephanie tried to focus to understand. She was too frightened to comprehend half of what Juana was saying. Her mind refused to think in Spanish.

"*Juana, despacio. No comprendo*. No understand."

"Go to beach. Go to city lights. In 5 kilometers is dirt road. You go in car there."

"What will you do? You must come with us!"

"No. I stay. It is my time for my," she paused. She did not know the word for *venganza* - revenge. "I go later. It okay. You go. Now. Must be quiet."

Stephanie found it impossible to stand. Her swollen feet were deeply bruised, and a stream of blood ran down her ankles from where the nylon strap had slowly been working its way into her skin. How could she walk that far? The excruciating pain made her tremble and perspire. "Juana, take Jere. I don't think I can make it. My legs. You go. Save Jere." A sob took her as she realized her fate.

"No, Senora Stephanie. You must go. Walk. You must go," Juana angrily commanded.

Stephanie could feel blood rushing into her lower extremities which now painfully tingled. Millions of tiny needles pricked her. It was unbearable to move her feet, let alone to stand upon them.

Sweat ran in rivers, completely drenching her. "Oh my god," she whispered more to herself than to Juana or Jere. "Please god! Help me!" She tried not to cry aloud, but the pain was crippling. How would she ever walk five kilometers down the beach?

Juana first tended to Jere and carefully helped her out the window where the quaking child hid in the shrubbery. Next she dragged Stephanie upright. Searing, white hot pain shot through her lower extremities. She thought she would faint.

"Now is no time for weakness, Senora. He dines upon the flesh of the weak. You must go. Pronto." Juana's voice, tense with urgency, became authoritative.

Before she could object, Juana half-carried her to the window. "You cry for pain later. Now, you must live. You go. NOW!" and the tiny savior sat her on the sill, spun her around, and lowered her into the bushes. "You go!"

***

Juana watched as Stephanie and Jere slowly crawled through the undergrowth along the side of the villa. Twenty feet from where she lowered them both to freedom, the path veered sharply right. There were no immediate doors or windows overlooking the path at that corner. She hoped Stephanie would have the sense to use that short space to cross left into the stand of palm trees where the two would quickly blend into the night.

She thought about joining them and running for her freedom, but to her, freedom no longer had meaning or value. With her children dead, her reason to live no longer existed in Juana's mind. The act of saving the lives of Stephanie and Jere repaid her debt to the detective who'd saved her life in the desert. If she died, her death would mean nothing to no one, but it would be for a good cause.

She would stay. She would exact her *venganza*, her revenge. If she lived, she would have to confess her sin so that she would not go to eternal hell with a mortal sin on her soul. But she feared even the padre in the confessional would betray her. She would have a price on her head. How could she escape the powerful men who would hunt her down? Better to burn in hell for eternity than to suffer their brutalities.

She was a survivor, and though the outlook appeared bleak, she nevertheless had prepared a plan for escape should luck befall her. In her handbag she carried a bus ticket that would get her to La Paz. At great expense she'd also purchased a ferry ticket that would transport her from La Paz to Puerto Vallarta. If she made it that far without being apprehended or robbed, she could get a bus to her final destination. She'd quickly be many miles from the crime scene if she could just escape the house after she committed the deed. The resort tips she'd saved over the last months funded her escape.

She watched Stephanie and Jere struggle across the path and into the palm grove. She felt certain that Stephanie would draw from inner strength to make the five kilometers. "*Vaya con Dios*," she whispered as she watched the two fugitives fade from view.

Now she would go to work. Should she approach him as he dined, or wait in his sleeping room? She quickly decided the dining room would be best for her appearance. She must, at all cost, keep him from wandering to check on Stephanie and Jere.

From her bag she took the apparel she'd given great thought to. She must dress and prepare her hair and face quickly. She didn't know how much time remained.

***

"Where we heading first?" Chloe asked as Starr sped down the narrow highway.

"Ben's waiting at the Fiesta Pacifica. I called him from the plane before we landed and told him to stay put - that we'd get him."

"Good. The more the merrier."

The two drove in silence for a distance, each thinking about the approaching assault.

"You got a plan?" Chloe finally asked.

"Hell, yes. That's what I get the big bucks for," Starr almost smiled.

"Hey, Marshal, I want you to know, I'm sorry about things. I shouldn't have snooped into your business. I intend to leave once Ben and his family are back in the States."

Jake Starr only looked at her. Chloe thought he might have nodded ever so slightly.

She looked out the window at the quickly darkening countryside. Good, she thought. Assaults at night were always more effective. Easier to get away in the dark too.

"Why you helping Ben anyway?"

"Why wouldn't I?"

"Well, like for starters, you're his primary suspect for the cactus murders."

Starr laughed. "My my. Never been a suspect before."

"Well, aren't you worried?"

"About?"

"About being arrested!"

"For what?"

"The murders! The cactus murders!" she said, exasperation creeping into her voice.

"Now why would I be worried about that?"

She looked at him, disbelief written on her face. If he was guilty, he definitely knew how to keep his cool.

"I buried my step-daughter and squashed the story of her death to protect my wife and my career. I am guilty of bad judgment, perhaps, but that's all. Ben will figure it out. He's smart."

"Do you know how Ben found out about your daughter?"

"I strongly suspect that Michael Lorenzo, aka Miguel Lorenzo south of the border, leaked the information to Stephanie Thomas, knowing full well she'd pass it on."

"Why would he do that?"

"Who the hell knows all the reasons he's drummed up. Miguel Lorenzo has been playing double agent for a long time – and a piss poor one at that. I think he gets easily confused nowadays trying to keep things straight. We just need to bring him up short. We don't reveal everything at our meetings when he's there, I'll tell you that much."

"So what are you going to do about it?"

"Oh, I'm thinking I might well arrest the gentleman once we're back in the states. Sweat him out. He'll break if we offer him a good deal. He's privy to information about the cartels that we need. There's something big happening."

Professionally she knew better than to ask for details. If Starr wanted her to know, he'd tell her. She switched gears. "So, you're just helping Ben then because you're a good guy?"

He didn't answer. Aha! Was it Stephanie Thomas he was helping? I'll probably never know that one, she thought as she watched the headlights piercing the darkness.

"Jake, will we be able to get out of here tonight, or will Lorenzo double-cross us?"

"Good question. I guess we'll find out." He smiled conspiratorially. "Exciting, huh?"

Oh shit! Just what I need right now, she thought. A twenty-year sentence in a Mexican jail.

She noticed her palms suddenly slick. When she glanced back at Starr, he was grinning, plainly enjoying her anxiety. Payback's hell, she grimaced.

***

As Ben feared, Juana did not materialize as promised at 7:00. "Damn her," he muttered as he returned from the entry security. "Damn her." He glanced for the umpteenth time at his watch as he took his post in front of the large, ornate entry to the Fiesta Pacifica. He waited impatiently for Starr and Chloe, pacing and continuously scanning the few cars that made it past the gatekeepers.

His Glock was secured in the back waistband of his pants. The Hawaiian shirt he'd bought one size too large was tucked in loosely so as not to show the weapon.

As Starr had directed, he was packed and ready to leave. He hadn't checked out. "Don't set off any alarms, Ben. Just load up your saddlebags and have them on the bike, ready to roll. If you've been watched, we don't want to give them any reason to suspect you may be leaving. If they think you're leaving, they'll know something's up since I'm sure they may know about Stephanie and Jere."

The plan was simple. Once Ben saw Starr and Chloe, he would get on his bike and follow the SUV, staying a few car lengths back. He'd follow them to the villa where they'd do the grab and run, and then head towards Todos Santos. Starr would radio ahead for the plane to warm up and to taxi to the runway. This assumed that Lorenzo didn't tip Passkey off. Starr seemed to think this wouldn't happen, that Lorenzo would choose to go with them. If he didn't choose to, they'd take him by force, or kill him, but Starr didn't volunteer this information.

Ben knew he would kill Passkey once he had Stephanie and Jere clear of the house, but he kept this part of the plan to himself.

"How quickly can you dismantle that machine you ride?" Starr asked Ben before he disconnected.

"Damn fast."

"Good. Just break it down far enough that we can load it. Hate to see a fine work of art like that left behind."

"To hell with the bike! I don't want to jeopardize our escape."

"No problem-o, I think the expression goes. We're good to go, Ben. You'll have time to tear it down if the *policia* don't show. If you can't, then leave it. Trust me, I don't want to jeopardize my safety. I don't think there's going to be a problem though."

"What makes you so sure about Lorenzo?"

"As of this moment, he's sitting in the plane, helping himself to liquor and cheap talk with the pilot."

"Good idea."

"It was the pilot's idea. Thank him when we get airborne. Meanwhile, we need to get off the air. See you in ten."

Had they talked too long and been intercepted? Ben didn't think so. How much of that went on down here anyway? Mexicans seemed so damned disorganized he couldn't imagine them having the technology to pick up cell phone calls. When it came to spying and war efforts, though, even the most backward countries always seemed to have the money and means to participate.

"Ah! Senior Franklin!" Ben saw a tall, distinguished man approach him, smile and extend his hand.

"Allow me to introduce myself. I am…"

Ben noticed him hesitate.

"I am Vincente Basilli. I saw your bike when you arrived and have been awaiting an opportunity to examine it with you present. I am a great admirer of the Harley Davidson."

The name rang a bell, and it took a moment until Ben remembered his conversation with Stephanie at Angelo's. What had she said? And he unconsciously squinted at Basilli, as though trying to remember where they'd met before.

"Haven't we met before?"

"I regret no. I would most certainly remember," Basilli answered suavely. "Because of the bike of course."

The man spoke with the tiniest accent, just a word here and there, but not an Italian accent. The more Ben looked at him, he could see Vincente Basilli was not Italian.

"Did we go to school together?" Ben asked, trying to dig for information.

"I attended school in the east."

"Oh, you just look familiar."

"So, you have done much custom work to your bike, I think," Basilli continued quickly, as if avoiding any possible connection between them.

"Yeah. I've added a few items," Ben said flatly, hoping to dissuade Basilli from examining the machine so he could watch uninterrupted for Chloe and Starr.

"Nice pipes. They must be loud?" Basilli smiled. "And what is this? A turbo charger?"

"Yep. She goes fast."

Basilli's admiration of the bike was genuine, Ben could see that. But this was not the time or place, and he had a gut feeling he should be arresting the man who was now gently stroking the gas tank on the V-Rod.

Basilli continued to ask about everything on the bike, including the saddlebags. Finally, "Well, when I return home perhaps I will purchase a Harley. But, the desert is inhospitable to these bikes I think. Too hot."

Alarms sounded. The desert? Immediately Ben realized what the discrepancy he was hearing in Basilli's speech was. The man was Arab, not Italian.

"So, you from Saudi? I was there once," Ben tried nonchalantly.

"Yes, well, I must leave. I am expected at someone's villa this evening. A night of great entertainment, I'm told. Perhaps I can talk with you at another time about the bike?"

"Sure thing," Ben answered as he mounted the cycle. He'd gotten a glimpse of Chloe and Starr as they'd slowed and honked outside the gates. "I'll catch you later."

The blast of the pipes was meant to shock Basilli and obviously hurt his ears, but he smiled gamely and walked away as Ben sped down the driveway to the intersection, falling in three cars behind the black SUV.

***

Ten steps later Basilli remembered where he'd seen Ben before. Most certainly it had been in the basement of the Bellagio where his uncle had been waylaid by two American thugs. Ben had been the detective assigned to the case. "Small world," he muttered, wondering if he should be worried about their prior encounter. Would the detective remember? He didn't think so, even still…

Chapter Sixteen

JUANA Salcedo stood before the full-length mirror and looked with dispassionate appraisal at the figure before her. Her delicate, childlike frame seemed too small to support the thick mane of high-lighted auburn hair which tumbled down the sides of her sculpted face. She did not see a beautiful young woman reflected in the mirror. She saw a well-used body, attractive to men who liked diminutive women, and eye-catching to pedophiles and pimps. She knew that her deliverance from prostitution was a blessing. Usually, young girls in the profession quickly passed through their prime and descended to hag-like remains. This much she had been spared.

The skirt rode low on her hips, tiny, tight, and seductively slit from the side of her thigh to the bottom of her hip bone. Just enough black thong showed. Her bared mid-riff, lean and taut, was loosely draped with an inexpensive, fine, gold-plaited chain. Her breasts were immodestly covered with a short, tight-fitting tank top clearly defining small nipples.

Her make-up and hair showed skillful application and arrangement. Her shoes, strappy, slutty, red spiked heels, added three inches to her stature, making her look easy and seductive. As she daubed a dime-store fragrance at the base of her throat, she finally drew the courage to look into her eyes. Looking back at her was an old woman, a woman who knew despair and hopelessness. The bag woman's eyes, haunted and ill, forcefully held her gaze.

For a brief moment, Juana caught her breath, shocked at the haggard orbs staring back at her. They harbored a sickness that went beyond misery of the soul. They looked careworn and fatigued, as though the person looking through them had grown weary of the world.

What had happened to her? All those years ago when her childhood was stolen in the night by the drunken, smelly, heavy man who rolled on top of her, crushing her tiny body, what had happened to the little girl inside? Where had she gone? After the first man, there were many, but it was only the first that mattered. Like a thief, he'd stolen her innocence, her childhood, her very self away, leaving her crushed, corrupted and defeated, a shell where once little Juana had lived, a happy quiet child, with warm, tender brown eyes and a shy, arresting smile.

Juana died the night she was molested and sodomized by the big, fat, sweaty ox of a man. Despite this, an almost invisible spark of tenderness and hope erupted inside the vacant casing of her body when her children were born, but then they too were taken from her in the scorching Arizona desert. She'd only wanted to give them a chance to survive and to escape from the savage world she knew. She didn't want her baby daughter violently ripped as she'd been. She didn't want her son to become a boy of the streets, a gang boy who would die many years before his time, or who would be shot in the spine and paralyzed, leading to a slow torturous death in a country that didn't support invalids. Now there were no sparks left. Her small flicker of a flame, completely extinguished by Bill Passkey, left her a dead woman in a barely living, skeletal frame.

Her time would come, she hoped quickly. She knew of her infection with HIV – the American hospital had sent a bi-lingual aide to advise her of her condition, but she didn't know of the cancer slowing moving through her cervix to the other organs of her wasting body. Too many sexual partners. Too little medical care. Too much misery.

She straightened, and for a moment her face grew haughty and hard. Pride prevented tears. Anger directed her to leave the specter she saw reflected in the mirror. But there was one last article, and she relished it as she carefully slid the sheathed straight razor into the back waistband of her lacy thong panty. Hardness now overcame her visage, and Juana Salcedo left the room, afraid of no one and nothing, not even death.

She stood quietly in the cool hallway, a calming breeze flowing through the open veranda doors, and she could hear raucous laughter coming from the other side of the house. She easily distinguished two voices. One belonged to a foreigner, not American. He spoke English fluently, but she detected an occasional inflection that was not that of a native speaker. The other voice belonged to Bill Passkey. Loud, crude, rough, filled with cursing and hostility. She braced herself for a moment. "I can do this," she muttered with steely resolve. "It will be over quickly." She crossed herself as she slowly made her way in the direction of the rowdy laughter.

***

For the first two kilometers, Stephanie wept in pain and worry that she and Jere would be discovered. She tried to keep her stops to a minimum, but the constant throbbing that hammered her was all but unbearable. She wondered what kind of irreparable damage she was causing herself with each excruciating step.

Beside her, bestowing support and encouragement, Jere performed like a war-wise trooper. "You can do it, Mom. Come on. Don't think about the pain," the young girl counseled. "Think about something else you really, really like. Like ice cream."

"Who taught you that?" Stephanie asked, a smile briefly visiting her lips. She already knew where Jere would get such sage advice.

"Dad did. He said that you can control almost everything in your body if you concentrate and like talk to your subconscious about it."

"Oh, he did, did he? Well, he's probably right. I feel better already just thinking about a hot fudge sundae," Stephanie tried not to gasp aloud as needle like sensations shot up her calf.

"I think it would be better, Mom, if you bent over more. Maybe we should walk closer to the palm trees – instead of so much in the open."

Stephanie saw that they had indeed wandered closer to the water. The hard packed sand along the shore was easier for her to hobble on, and she thought that if they stopped for just a bit and she soaked her legs they might feel better. But her daughter's reasoning was sound, so she reluctantly let Jere lead her closer to the fringe of palms.

"Mom, do you think Dad will find us?"

"Yes, Jere. Your Daddy will come."

"I hope he hurries up." Jere's intense expression spoke volumes.

They walked in silence, Stephanie's mind tracing over the week with Ben. She could not go through with it. She couldn't. Ben would see through her deception in a minute, if he hadn't already. She'd invited him to Cabo to manipulate him into giving her joint custody of Jere. It killed her to think of the horrendous mistake made years ago when she stormed out, petulant and pouty at his lack of response to her wiles and conniving. She looked at the exquisite child beside her who attempted to guide her by the elbow, and she wanted to throw herself on the ground and beg forgiveness. She had to. What if they didn't make it? Jere had to know.

"Jere," Stephanie began, a painful lump filling her throat, tears quickly forming.

"Yes, Mommy?"

"Jere, let's stop a minute," and Stephanie dropped to her knees, grabbing her daughter around the waist, holding her head. "Jere, I am so sorry, baby."

"What for, Mommy?" the startled, frightened girl asked.

"Jere, please forgive me," and sobs washed through her.

"Mommy, what's wrong," the child's voice shook.

"I am so sorry, honey, that I have not been here for you. That I left you and Daddy. Jere, I made a terrible mistake. A terrible mistake. I am so sorry." She let the flood of tears rage. For a full minute neither spoke as Stephanie clung to the child as a drowning person might cling to her rescuer.

"It's okay, Mommy. Don't cry." She felt Jere's small, warm hand pat her maternally on the back, but she didn't know the confusion raging through the little girl who was not certain how far her largess should extend.

"I love you, Jere. I always have. I just want you to know that. Never doubt it for a minute." Stephanie slowly arose, wiping her eyes and smiling weakly at her daughter.

"I love you too, Mommy, but why did you go away?"

"It was foolish of me. I made a bad decision. I'm so sorry. Someday maybe I can tell you about it, try to explain it. But I was wrong. There's no excuse. No explanation is good enough. I was so wrong, and I'm so, so sorry."

She sensed Jere's confusion and stopped proclaiming her undying love. She knew her daughter loved her, but she knew also that Jere's fealty to her father was strong. Could Jere ever love them both the same? She saw worry crease her daughter's brow. She knew her daughter fretted about her dad's feelings, and she didn't want to cause her baby girl such confusion and consternation.

The two held hands as they slowly made their way through the coconut grove. Stephanie had no idea how far they had traveled, but she hoped if they were in the woods, they might see the car or the road better than walking along the beach.

To help distract from the pain stabbing at her feet, they played little guessing games, each trying to be light-hearted for the benefit of the other. Stephanie often shushed Jere, fearful they'd be overheard and apprehended.

"Dad would say not to think of the journey as five kilometers, but just to think of walking 100 steps. Then he'd say to think of the next 100 after you did the last one. He says it's easier to break things down sometimes than to look at the whole picture."

"Yes, I can believe he would say that," Stephanie smiled as much as her pain allowed.

"Well, I'm going to use the power of my subconscious and get us safe," the little girl spoke with authority and conviction.

What other delightfully esoteric things would Ben have taught her, Stephanie wondered. She did not deserve to ask him for joint custody. She should be happy with what he graciously had granted her. She felt as sick at heart as she did in body.

"Mommy, would you rather have power or magic?" Jere asked unexpectedly, saving her from more self-imposed berating.

"Hmmm. I'll have to think about that one."

"Tell me when you decide."

Despite herself, Stephanie found herself pondering the merits of power versus magic. "I think magic would be fun, but to be honest, I have to choose power."

"Not me. I'd choose magic, because then I could trick all the people in power."As she smiled at Jere's reasoning, her pain momentarily subsided. "I suppose that's true." She realized her choice of power came from her need for approval, praise, control and respect. Those things might not be benefits to someone who possessed magic. But power…was that what this was all about with Ben? She knew she had the power to force him into a joint custody arrangement, and she'd planned to do so if she couldn't get her way with him in Cabo. Oddly, Ben had all the power she craved, and yet he never resorted to it.

"Mommy, what's infinity?"

"Well, it's a hard concept to understand, Jere. I don't know that I can explain it right now."

"Dad told me it was a number so big, so humongous, that nobody in the whole wide world knows what it is."

"He did, did he?"

"But then I asked him what was the number right before the infinity number and he just shook his head."

Suddenly the ground changed to rutted, hard-packed dirt. And both of them realized they'd come upon the road where Juana said they'd find a car. They'd made it. She hoped the car wasn't much further.

***

As mother and daughter made their way to the safety of a waiting vehicle, Juana Salcedo came to a standstill in the arched entryway of the elaborate dining room, her hand on one hip, the other hip jutting slightly forward. She summoned a provocative stare and posed twenty feet from Passkey, watching the beast shovel a forkful of chicken into his already half-full mouth. At the other end of the table Vincente Basilli sat, his manners impeccable, his bearing regal as he watched, disgusted, as Passkey greedily masticated his food. He sensed Juana's presence a few moments before Passkey, who was busily sopping up salsa and cheese with a tortilla and thinking of the mother and daughter, bound and waiting.

The girl was beautiful beyond belief. Slender, shapely, and sexually expressive. Was this the dessert Passkey had alluded to on the telephone? Basilli felt himself growing warm, his pulse quickening. He thought the young woman too exquisite to be a whore, but she had to be. He hoped he could take her to the hotel, for she was too precious to be fouled by the disgusting, rank miscreant sitting across from him. Silence from Passkey's end of the table startled him back to his senses.

He saw Passkey sitting stupefied, a mixture of lust, disbelief, and love dancing across his unshaven face. Neither man spoke as Juana sidled forward, allowing Passkey's eyes to caress each part of her undulating body. Still silent, she stood beside him and unhurriedly extended her slender hand to stroke the man's ruddy, pitted face. Pursing her lips slightly, she bent, whispering, "Would you like me to dance for you, amigo?" She breathed heavily into his ear, and his face flushed with desire, his breath labored.

From the other end of the table, Basilli watched in horror as the abominable Passkey reached out and grabbed the girl by her hips, pulling her roughly onto his lap. "You little whore, where the hell you been all this time?" he muttered, his hands running rampant over her body.

"Perhaps I should come back another time," Basilli began, but Passkey merely waved him off.

"Nonsense. I'll be right with you. Excuse us for a moment," and he stood, swaying slightly. Basilli watched him sling Juana over his shoulder and wink lewdly as he carried her out of the room. Basilli knew the loathsome bastard was planning all the ways he might heap indignity upon indignity onto the young woman who had obviously tantalized and tormented him.

Even though the silence in the room was almost palpable after Passkey left, it was some minutes before Basilli heard the help as they slunk about gathering dishes and scowling in the direction Passkey had carried Juana. He could see that she was one of them, and that they hated the thought of the man ravishing the young woman who had already suffered enough.

"I'll be leaving. Please get my jacket and call for my car," Basilli said to no one in particular, standing up from the table, disappointed that the girl would not be his. Perhaps when Passkey was finished? He didn't think so. It was then he recognized her as the same girl who had come to the hotel in search of Ben. Was she Ben's concubine?

He summoned his driver on his cell phone and decided, wisely, to wait outside. He did not want to be privy to Passkey's carnal grunts and groans, which he was sure the beast of a man would release. Nor did he hear Passkey's blood curdling screams as Basilli's limousine exited onto the highway forty-five minutes later. He was not there to watch as Juana, bathed in the blood of her tormentor, walked into the night, conveniently not seen by anyone in the household, all of whom happened to be otherwise engaged.

It was some minutes before any of the house staff entered Bill Passkey's room. They hoped the silence meant he was dead. Instead they found the man laying on blood soaked sheets, in shock, holding a testicle and his severed penis in his hand. Each servant fought to suppress a smile of gratitude.

***

The car started on the first turn of the key, and Stephanie and Jere smiled at each other, relief washing over them, hope fully rising on the horizon with the full moon.

Chapter Seventeen

THERE are those who say there is no such thing as coincidence, that there are simply times when the forces of nature come together and conspire to produce events often mislabeled as coincidental. Others insist that fate determines one's outcome. Some call it predestination. Some, luck. Some even call it God's divine will, the same will that launches tsunamis on unsuspecting islanders, demolishes entire towns with tornados, visits continents with drought, condemns innocents with AIDS, and threatens flood and fire. Coincidence, fate, cosmic forces, and divine will all offer an explanation, answer, and hope…or despair.

As Stephanie and Jere navigated the dark, curvy highway, both sat silent, attentive to meandering livestock along the roadway and praying the dilapidated vehicle would not die. On this route, cars were scarce, so both grew rigid with fear as the headlights of an upcoming vehicle flashed upon them. A limousine traveling at dangerously high speed passed without slowing, allowing them to resume breathing. Both looked askance at each other, tension mounting.

The unlit, deserted, narrow road snaked dangerously through the Mexican countryside. Livestock and large potholes alternately presented themselves as obstacles as the old jalopy, with a solitary headlight, coughed and lurched, carrying the fleeing fugitives to Cabo.

They drove with the windows down and the warm desert air filling the rusty car. The car's handles had long ago broken free, so rolling windows up for protection should Passkey find them was not an option. They traveled in silence, Jere perched on the edge of the seat next to her mother, eyes glued to the road ahead.

"Mommy!" she looked at her mother, her eyes widening.

"What, Jere? What is it?"

"Mommy! It's Daddy. Can't you hear it?"

And then she heard the unmistakable rumble of the Harley's custom pipes. Frantically she searched for the high beams and the horn. Neither worked. Madly she pushed on the center of the steering wheel. The pipes were almost upon them. She screamed out the window as she slammed on the brakes as a black SUV and the Harley roared by. The door. She couldn't open the door. "BEN! BEN! HELP!" She screamed as the taillights rounded a bend.

Beside her, Jere's little voice pierced the darkness."Daddy! Come back! Daddy!"

Hysteria drowned her reason, and Stephanie alternately screamed and sobbed as she battered her already bloody hands trying to force the door.

As Stephanie's desperation swallowed her, terror engulfed Jere. Stephanie saw her scramble out the window and run in the direction of the disappearing bike. Beating mercilessly on her own door, she watched as her daughter ran screaming, terror-stricken and frenzied up the middle of the dark highway. The door finally popped free with a loud grating screech and Stephanie fell onto the pavement. She saw Jere turn to see her prone, and then she saw her freeze. Stephanie knew the girl was unable to decide whether to race after the safety of her father, or to return to her as she raised herself on bloody knees, calling out, gulping, choking, pleading, "Jere, come back. We'll go find Daddy together. Come back."

Suddenly the roar was again upon them, and Ben, skidding and leaping from the bike, swept his daughter into his arms, the Harley sliding to a silent repose in the roadway. Minutes later the SUV's headlights found Stephanie, Jere, and Ben wrapped in an embrace alongside the dangerous, desert highway.

***

Juana left the bed of her rapist without looking at her handiwork. Despite his horrific, ear piercing screams, she calmly retrieved her belongings and walked casually across the back veranda and down the steps onto the cool sand.

The evening breeze dried the perspiration gathered at her hairline and she stood a moment, a bit shaky, before she coolly walked to the water's edge, dropped her belongings and waded into the cleansing waters of the Pacific. The bottom dropped off sharply, and she struggled to keep her head above water, but soon rolled to her back, relaxing as her hair billowed, halo-like, around her. Thin though she was, it took only a minimum of effort to stay afloat in the warm saltwater, and she allowed the current and swell to move her peacefully about.

The stars shone brilliantly, and she was reminded of the night sky that had hidden her in the Arizona desert. Would the stars looking down upon her now in her victory be the same ones that had watched her struggle in ignominy those many months ago?

She didn't feel as good as she thought she'd feel after slicing through Bill Passkey. Certainly she did not feel worse, but she didn't have the feeling of euphoria that she supposed she would have. But it was good. The deed was done. He would probably die from blood loss. If he lived, even better. And she smiled thinking of his well-deserved fate.

Slowly she made her way back to shore and emerged from the healing water; a feeling of serenity filled her. She would dress and head north. There were bus stops along the highway. She would ride the next north bound bus. If luck was on her side, she would make it to La Paz and thence to Puerto Vallarta. If not, so be it. Momentarily she wondered if she should check on the mother and daughter. Did they make it to the car? Did the old beater carry them to safety? No, she would go on her way. Their threat was now indisposed, and she never doubted that Ben would find them.

She heard commotion coming from down the beach and knew someone had found Passkey. She smiled and dressed quickly. Police would come. Best to be gone. She hummed quietly as she walked quickly up the beach, each footstep freeing her from the hell that had been Bill Passkey.

***

Ben carried Stephanie up the steps of the waiting plane, with Jere clinging tightly to his arm.

"Lay her in the back, Ben," Chloe directed as she retrieved an onboard emergency medical kit.

Gently he lowered Stephanie onto a small settee, anger and grief vying for his immediate response. The entire left side of her face was swollen and bruised. Her puffy eye opened only a slit. Blood streaks ran the length of her face and neck, settling in the white cotton of her shirt.

Fury raged in him. He'd kill the bastard, and he turned to leave the plane when Jere grabbed him, burying her face in his stomach.

"Daddy, don't leave me. Please."

He felt her shake in fright as she clung maniacally to him. He glanced up to see Chloe approach with the medical supplies.

"Better help Starr get your bike torn apart. He's hell bent to bring that thing, one way or the other."

He looked out the cabin window to see Starr and the pilot dismantling the bike at break neck speed as Lorenzo stood uselessly looking on. Parts flew off as Starr expertly wielded ratchets and other tools.

"Get the feeling he doesn't want you to stay?" Chloe asked, moving past him to the supine woman. "Forget about going after him now, Ben. This is not the time. You'll get your shot at him. Starr will see to it. You leave us now you put all of us in danger, including your wife and child." He did not seem to notice the reference to Stephanie as his wife.

He sat Jere in a seat, grabbing her a blanket and pillow. "Daddy, don't go," and the girl burst into tears again.

"Jere, look out the window. I'll be right there. I'll be back. I'm not going." Still he could feel her grip. The child would not release him. "Jere, I have to go help. Stay with your mom. I'll be right there. You can see me the whole time," and he tore himself from her.

He heard her screams as he scurried down the plane's steps. "Daddy! Come back!" He'd kill the bastard who'd caused such terror.

Within minutes the three men wrestled the bike into the plane, and taxied down the short runway. They would be flying again without a flight plan or permission over a foreign country, but the odds of pursuit were slim, and the pilot would keep the plane low over the Sea of Cortez.

"I've radioed ahead, Ben. There'll be an ambulance waiting when we land."

He nodded in response, holding Jere on his lap as the little girl sobbed herself to sleep.

***

Formerly trained as a paramedic during her work with the Alaska state troopers, Chloe knew to treat Stephanie for shock as much as anything else. She quickly assessed the woman's injuries, and saw that none were life-threatening although there would definitely be some scarring. Her cheekbone was most likely fractured, and the odds were good that she might always have some degree of discomfort in her feet and lower legs. Perhaps not. She found herself hoping not.

"You'll be okay, Stephanie," she spoke quietly. "You're going to be okay. A few little scars. Nothing serious. In a few days you'll be out and about."

Stephanie mustered a weak smile. "Thank you."

Both women were silent as Chloe cleaned the dirt and sand from the ligature marks on Stephanie's ankles.

"Chloe, I…"

"Shh. You shouldn't talk."

"No. I want to tell you…" Stephanie bit her lip and fell silent.

"I know. Don't worry." After a moment of silence, Chloe continued. "He still loves you. You know that, don't you?" She was surprised when Stephanie shook her head no.

"I don't know why he would."

"He loves you. He's never stopped loving you."

"But, what about you?"

"Ben never loved me. He made a mistake bringing me here to Arizona. It was a good move for me, but a mistake for him. There was never really anything between us." She laughed quietly. "He even called me Stephanie several times."

Chloe saw tears well in Stephanie's eyes and knew from her own recent experience that the woman thought back to the years that had passed, years that Ben had continued to love her, years she had appeared too self-involved to care. Chloe sighed, knowing that Stephanie had made that all too familiar mistake of waiting for him to crawl back to her. Now she must crawl to him and beg him to take her back. It was a scenario Chloe knew well, having just done the same with Mack when she finally broke down and visited him in Papeete.

"Are you sure? That he still loves me?"

"No doubt about it."

Chloe closed the medical bag and prepared to leave.

"Thank you. Thank you for everything. For taking care of him. For caring for him. For telling me."

She smiled. "Get some rest, Stephanie. And you don't need to go crawling back. He'll take you in a heartbeat. He loves you. Don't forget that."

***

Juana sat in the small bus shelter, shivering in the morning air. She had not thought to pack food, and hunger gnawed at her. She hadn't felt hunger in a long while - not since that moment that time had stopped for her.

She dozed, her head periodically jerking her back to wakefulness. She yawned and stood. It would not do to sleep. She must stay alert and keep an eye for the *policia*, should they be searching, which she doubted. All men hated Passkey, but they would hate what she had done to him even more. She smiled to herself. Her debt to Ben was paid. Her revenge on Passkey complete. Yes. She felt better.

Death in the Desert

As the sun rose a cock crowed, and a green and white bus appeared on the horizon. It would be a good day. And she would eat in a restaurant in La Paz.

Chapter Eighteen

ALL were silent on the short return flight, each lost in worrisome thoughts, thankful that the kidnapping had been resolved without bloodshed, but knowing that unspoken business remained.

Chloe sighed as she looked at the moon reflected on the beautiful sea below. Soon she would be seeing a lot of sea, and she smiled in anticipation. As much as she wanted to leave immediately, she needed to attend to things…details. Since it was possible she might never return to the United States, she needed to see her parents and brothers for what might be one last time. There was the stupid apartment that had to be closed up, her possessions donated, financial arrangements made. The list of to-do's seemed interminable. "I'll start tomorrow," she chided herself. "No more delays. No more assignments. I'm outta here." She'd pick a date and stick to it and leave regardless of whether things were finished or not. "I'll buy my ticket! That'll do the trick." She smiled as she picked a date. "April 19th sounds good. I'll buy a ticket for April 19th and that's it," she whispered happily. It gave her four months. She'd write Mack immediately and tell him she would soon be by his side. After all the years and tears, she would no longer deny her love for the man who left her in Alaska. Who would take the cat?

She was deeply relieved to be leaving Mexico without having fired a shot or having been involved in hand to hand combat. Her stiffening back and tender throat would have hampered her. The rescue of Stephanie and Jere could have been dicey – and could easily have turned deadly. She was curious how the two escaped their captor, but Stephanie was in no condition to talk.

***

Jake Starr again sat in the co-pilot seat while Bud Lewinsky flew hot and heavy for the border. "Reminds me a bit of 'Nam," Lewinsky said, excitement showing in his eyes.

Starr smiled in response. The two men went back more than thirty years to Vietnam. Lewinsky had flown copters while Starr ran boats up and down the Mekong Delta. They'd met in a Saigon bar, argued about whose professional baseball team was better, and fought afterwards until they both collapsed, well-bloodied. They'd formed an unlikely friendship that night and had remained in contact for the next three decades, calling for favors when needed, periodically sharing the successes and sorrows of life's passage. This episode would be another memory for the two to share.

Lewinsky flew as a private pilot, and Starr knew the flight tonight was compliments of the unsuspecting corporation that paid Bud a royal salary. The company would never be apprised of the plane and pilot's unscheduled adventure. Starr watched as Lewinsky handled the controls, a smile stretching across his face.

His own thoughts revolved around Lorenzo – and Ben. He didn't care how Stephanie had escaped, he was just relieved that he hadn't had to shed blood on Mexican soil. But he was deeply disturbed by Lorenzo. Why had the man given information to Stephanie Thomas? What had motivated him? Obviously it was to discredit him, but why? What would Lorenzo get from it? It wasn't like Lorenzo was in line for his job. It had to be a set-up, pure and simple. If he could figure out why, he could proceed. He just could see no benefit in any of this for his betrayer.

The man was a snake. Starr had never liked nor trusted him, but had never thought him particularly dangerous.

"What'd you and Lorenzo chat about?" Starr asked.

"Women mostly. Dope. Money that can be made from women and dope. That man loves his dope. No specifics."

"Did he mention any names? Places?"

"Not really. He asked how much a plane like this would cost. Said he thought it would pay for itself if he could load it with crop. Said it would beat the hell out of the commercial runs."

Starr thought for a bit. "That's what he said? Commercial runs?"

"Yeah. That was pretty much it."

Were the drugs coming in on commercial airlines? "Anything else?"

"Now that I think about it, he did say this Passkey was a real bad ass. Said he hoped you blew him away."

Starr sat silent a moment.

"Hope we got enough fuel," he heard Lewinsky comment offhandedly.

"What the hell does that mean?"

"Well, we didn't start out with exactly full tanks, and we're carrying a lot of weight back what with the bike, Lorenzo, Ben, and the two gals we picked up. Not to mention we're flying low and hot."

"Good grief. You got any more good news?"

***

Ben focused on breathing, matching his own breath to Jere's as she slowly relaxed as sleep overcame her. He closed his eyes but saw only his daughter looming in the headlights of his bike. His heart involuntarily pounded each time the vision of the terrified child appeared. He kept seeing her, barefoot and crying, with Stephanie on the pavement, bloody and battered. His throat constricted and his back arched and stiffened. "Damn him. I'll kill him," he swore as pure hatred gripped him.

I can't go on like this, he thought. It's got to stop. My daughter could have died. Stephanie could have died. This job is not worth their lives. It costs too much.

He knew obsession with his job had cost him his marriage. Tonight it had almost cost him the only thing that kept him from the edge – his daughter. When had he last held her like this?

He swore he would leave the force. He'd settle the Cactus Murder case and leave. He'd find something else. Something safe. Fun. Something he could live in the country doing. He'd buy Jere a horse. She wanted a horse in the worst way. He stroked the little girl's silky, auburn hair. He'd find something to do. Not the law. No more. It asked too much.

He closed his eyes and tried to envision a country home with a horse in the back yard, but even as the image appeared, it was marred by the visage of Bill Passkey. He'd kill Passkey first. Then he would start over. Reinvent himself. That was Stephanie's term for it.

He thought about her urging him to go to school. "I never see you do art work anymore, Ben. You could be brilliant. You did beautiful sculpture work. Why don't you go back and do something with your god-given talent?"

He hadn't created since he began hunting people down.

The Cactus Murders first. Passkey second. He would begin a new life then. He had to finish up. He couldn't leave the table with a mess on it. So, was Starr the cactus murderer? And what about Betsy Brunkee? Had Chloe located her? And where did Lorenzo fit in this evil stew?

How the hell could he arrest Starr after this? He owed the man. Was that the reason Starr had come roaring in like a posse? Or was there another reason, and Ben unexpectedly felt a twinge of jealousy stir as he thought of Stephanie and her work on the task force. He suddenly remembered the last meeting and Starr sitting next to her, talking to her afterwards as Ben rushed from the room, steaming at the unexpected drubbing he'd received. Well, she wasn't his wife anymore, and he had no doubt she would blame the kidnapping on his past pursuit of Passkey and the past drug case in Juneau that he'd assisted Chloe with. He blamed himself. It was natural she would too. If Stephanie was the impetus for Starr's rescue efforts, all the more reason for Ben to get the hell out of Dodge.

Despite his internal war over the pile of guilt descending on him, he finally dozed fitfully, dreaming of a little girl on a horse in a large meadow. But when the horse turned toward him, it wore Bill Passkey's face.

***

Stephanie's pain subsided, and the anxiety eased, but still she lay tormented, turning over Chloe's unexpected words. Were they so unexpected really? If she were honest with herself, deep down she knew that Ben still cared for her. It leaped from his face every time they met. Love blossomed in his beautiful gray eyes despite his efforts to squash the delicate message. He was a good man. She didn't deserve him.

She didn't believe in fairy-tales and "things working out." She was educated and pragmatic. She'd made the mistake of her life; there was no way he'd ever trust her again. She'd never trust anyone if they'd done to her what she'd done to Ben.

For several years she rationalized her departure, blaming his job and the long hours he dedicated to his profession. "That is what men do, Stephanie," her mother once told her after an evening of heart-to-heart. "They work. Pity the woman whose husband does not love his work. There you will find the panderer, the alcoholic, the critic."

Her mother was old-fashioned. What would she know? She had catered to her father for over forty years, humoring his whims and passions, yet undeniably waltzing through life to her own music. She made it look so easy – and fun. Stephanie took pride in being much smarter than most women, her mother included. Why couldn't she be happy – like her mother? She loved Ben. Why couldn't she just say it?

If Chloe was right and Ben still loved her… Her thoughts slowly flowed from her, ebbing like the tide until her guilty, berated conscience would again prick her to a flood of tears and the painful memory of her mistake. Finally, she was lulled to sleep by the drone of the plane's engine and the effects of the Demerol that Chloe had administered.

***

Miguel Lorenzo anxiously chewed at the cuticle of his thumb nail. He looked worriedly about the plane as though still deciding whether he should board the craft or not. He'd stood on the runway, momentarily paralyzed as to whether he should go with the Americans or purposefully stride to his vehicle and drive home, feigning ignorance of the re-capture of the woman and the girl when grilled by Passkey. He still didn't know that Starr and the woman cop had taken no action. He assumed they had obtained the release of the two. He didn't want to bear the brunt of Passkey's rage and ensuing assault, so he'd meekly acquiesced when ordered by Starr to board the plane. When he thought about it now that he had calmed himself, he realized that he had, in fact, been commanded by Starr, and he had no doubt that the marshal would've used force if necessary to ensure his obedience.

He must think. Why would Starr take him unless he suspected that he'd given the information to Stephanie about Betsy Brunkee. Lorenzo tried to recall the hurried conversation as the lawman approached on the plane, but he couldn't resurrect the details, only that Starr had indicated he knew about the folder. What precisely had the man said? He wanted physically to pound his head, as though the answer might be stuck and could be dislodged. Too rattled to waste time dredging his drug-damaged memory, he decided to assume the worst – that Starr knew he'd given the information to Stephanie Thomas, who Lorenzo had correctly assumed would pass it on to the big detective.

He could see why Passkey feared the cop. There was a purposefulness in the man's eyes, and a determination in the way he moved. He didn't doubt that the cop would kill in an instant if so motivated.

Having bloodied his thumb, he advanced to the index finger and began gnawing. The cocaine was waning.

Betsy Brunkee. Lorenzo closed his eyes and again saw the stupendously beautiful seventeen-year-old. What had grabbed his attention was her hair. She had the thickest, heaviest, finest, blondest hair he'd ever seen. Just looking at it made him reach out to stroke the mixture of golden, yellow, and white strands, somehow so woven as to be the most astounding and magnificent color he'd ever imagined.

She'd come to Starr's office looking for him to take her to lunch. Lorenzo knew Starr would return momentarily, apologized for her father's delay and told her that he was her substitute luncheon date. The girl hesitated, wary. She was a lawman's daughter. She wouldn't be easy to convince, so he turned on his Latin charm.

"I am offended that I alarm you, senorita," he crooned, giving a winsome, boyish smile.

"No. No, I'm not scared. It's just that he didn't say anything about…" she said in a faltering voice.

"I'll tell you what we'll do. To put your mind at ease…we'll leave him a note inviting him to join us. Does that make you easier?"

He could see it did not make it easier, and she stood, uncertain what to say or do.

"Come. We'll eat right here in the building. The food is horrible, but your comfort is more important."

"No, I'll just wait for…"

"Suit yourself, senorita. You will have a long wait, I fear."

"I'll go home, I guess. I'll see him tonight probably."

"As you wish," and he opened the door for her, leaning in towards her as she passed from the room.

The elevator opened as she left the office, and Starr appeared, an uncustomary smile suddenly creasing his face. He wrapped his arm about her, turned, and the two disappeared into the elevator.

Smitten, Lorenzo began stalking the girl. For weeks he obsessed over the blonde Madonna, finding several excuses to appear at the family ranch, and stopping by the townhouse in Scottsdale on occasion to drop off pointless communiqués. Always his eyes searched frantically for a glimpse of the blonde beauty.

He followed her regularly, keeping several car lengths back, as she roamed the greater Phoenix area malls and cinema complexes, always with a bevy of precocious teenagers. On more than one occasion he sat behind the flock of them in a theatre, and it excited him to reach out surreptitiously and lightly touch her hair during the stultifying teen flicks that the girls found irresistible.

Then, miraculously she came again to her father's office when Starr was absent.

"My friends think you're cute," her coy little manner gripped his heart.

"Your friends? Do I know any of your friends?"

"I pointed you out to them once when I saw you at the movies."

"Hmm. What movie was that?"

"I don't remember. We go all the time. Anyway, they thought you were cute."

"And do you think I'm cute, as they say?"

"Mmm. Maybe. A little bit." He watched her as she moved to a chair by his desk, unconsciously tossing her mane of hair back while crossing her long, tan legs.

He didn't want to move too quickly. He had to make sure she was hooked before he reeled her in.

"So, what can I do for you today, Miss…?"

"You can call me Betsy if you want."

"Thank you, Miss Betsy. What can I do for you?"

"Well, since my dad's not here, you could take me to lunch," she said as he watched a flirtatious smile cross her face.

"Well, let me see if I can fit you in," he winked at her and pretended to look through his day calendar. "I think I can manage," he said after a moment. To add importance to his declaration, he dialed his home phone and spoke to the answering machine. "This is Michael Lorenzo at the U.S. Marshal's Office. Something's come up. I need to cancel. Tell Mr. Jones that I will reschedule him – or my secretary will reschedule him for a later time."

It excited him beyond belief to put his hand on the small of her back as he guided her into the elevator and then to his car.

"Wow. A cool car. My dad won't let me have a sports car. I have to drive that boat of an old beater."

"Well, a sports car is dangerous on these freeways. Your car is much safer if you are in a wreck." He could not control his hand as it reached out and tucked a wisp of her hair behind her ear.

Returning his attention to the wheel, he grew embarrassed and began to sweat.

"You sound just like him. Do all adults practice being practical, or is it just lawmen?"

He smiled, relieved that his advance did not draw a negative reaction.

"Where we going?"

"Oh – I'll take you somewhere special. Somewhere I bet you've never been before."

"Okay. But I gotta tell ya, we eat out all the time, so if it's a restaurant, I've probably eaten there."

"Your mother doesn't cook?"

"Yeah. She cooks once in a while. But she works a lot with the horses. She shows horses. Trains them and all that kind of stuff. Sometimes Lucinda cooks for us. She's a good cook."

"And Lucinda is…?"

"Our housekeeper. She mostly lives on the ranch. Sometimes she comes to Scottsdale to clean and stuff."

"Hmm. Well, I have to make one stop, if that's all right with you."

"Oh, sure. My mom's away at a horse show, and my dad thinks I'm still at the ranch, so I'm free for the day." Her innocent smile caused his heart to flutter.

He didn't have a plan. He never dreamed his obsession would come to fruition, and now he found himself floundering. "I must swing by my house for just one moment to get some important papers for court."

"Okay."

"You can wait in the car if you prefer. But be certain to keep the doors locked. My neighborhood has had a rash of savage rapes and assaults lately."

"Uh, if it's okay, I'll just wait inside your door. If it's alright."

"Of course. But you will see how a messy bachelor lives."

"That's cool." Her happy laugh made him laugh too.

They chatted aimlessly as he drove not to his house, but to the home of Roberto Vasquez – a prominent Mexican importer of beautiful handmade artifacts, and cocaine. He knew Vasquez would be at work in his large emporium and hoped he wouldn't mind him stopping briefly. Vasquez did mind, however, when he found Lorenzo wringing his hands over the dead teen.

"I just wanted to have her once, Roberto," he cried. "Just one time I wanted to run my fingers through her hair and see her naked body. She would never have consented. I only thought a bit of the liquid extract in her drink would smooth the way," he continued to bawl.

"You fool! You fool! Get out! Take your dead girlfriend with you! Don't come to my house again, Miguel. You have jeopardized us all! You have put the entire operation at risk! Get out! Take the blonde bimbo and get out."

Three days later Betsy Brunkee was found dead in the back bedroom of a known meth house. Blunt scissors had hacked her beautiful hair off at the nape of her neck. He kept the bundle of foot long hair tied with a piece of ribbon in a bedroom drawer.

The memento gave him great pleasure, although the thought of the girl's death often made him panicky and anxious.

Now he suddenly knew he had to get back to Mexico. The sooner the better. He'd never survive under Starr's scrutiny.

Miles of desert floor lay below the descending plane. He'd escape into the desert tonight if necessary. He realized that if Passkey had been eliminated from the action that night by the Americans in their rescue attempt, there would be any number of people willing to give him up in retaliation for their loss of drug revenue. Passkey, despicable though he was, had a way of making things happen – of bringing people and forces together. Surely some disgruntled drug supplier would give him up, and then only god could save him from the wrath of Jake Starr, and he knew that at this point in his life, god would never come to his rescue.

Chapter Nineteen

THE last words Ben heard Starr say as the small group deplaned on the remote runway north of Lukeville were, “Tomorrow. My office. 10:00.” Occupied with Stephanie and Jere, he was only vaguely aware that Starr then ushered Lorenzo into his vehicle, leaving the four of them to ride in the ambulance and Bud Lewinski to unload the bike and to return the plane to a semblance of order. No one but Lewinsky knew they'd flown in on fumes. One engine had actually begun to sputter.

Despite protestations from the ambulance crew, Ben insisted they would all ride crowded into the tiny compartment with Stephanie. The silence in the vehicle was palpable as the paramedic performed his ministrations.

“I'll grab a cab back to Starr's to pick up my car,” Chloe said as they pulled up to the emergency entry. “I totally forgot I left it there.” Ben only nodded in response.

“Do you want me to take Jere?”

He looked to his daughter and saw her forcefully shake her head. “I want my mom.”

“She should probably stay for observation tonight,” he suggested, trying to ease Jere's rejection of Chloe's hospitality.

“It's okay. She probably should stay, you're right.” Pausing, she said, “Do you want me to meet with you and Starr tomorrow, Ben?”

He hesitated. The case was the last thing on his mind. He reminded himself he needed to talk with Chloe before he met with Starr.

"Let's meet at 9:00…in the cafeteria downstairs. I need to know what you found out."

"Okay. See you then," and he watched her as she headed to the entry to get a cab.

There were reports, papers, and more forms to fill out than he'd ever before seen, and he was a man familiar with arrest reports, booking forms, and all the endless paperwork inherent in his job. While he fumbled through the massive stack of documents, Stephanie and Jere were taken to a small, curtained cubicle. Finally, he found his way free to join the two patients.

As he entered the treatment room he smiled, expertly searching Stephanie's face in an effort to read a prognosis.

"They're going to keep me here overnight for observation, Ben. I'll be fine. Take Jere home. I'll get a cab tomorrow."

"Nonsense. I'll be here to pick you up."

"You have other matters to tend to. I'll get a cab. I'll be fine."

He hesitated. He didn't want to leave her alone after her ordeal. "Only if you stay at the house with Francesca to look after you. Otherwise no deal." He finally saw her smile.

"That would be nice. I'll be in Wickenburg when you get home."

He leaned over and gently kissed her on the forehead. "Sorry. I forget myself," he muttered as he straightened.

"Thank you, Ben." He felt her long slim fingers seek his strong, massive hand. He couldn't remember feeling anything so wonderful as she wrapped her hand around his. "Ben…"

"Shh. We'll talk later. Rest now. You're going to feel emotional because of your ordeal. It's normal. We'll talk when you're better."

"What I want to say won't change," he saw the agony on her beat up face as tears welled again.

"Mommy?" Jere appeared on the other side of the bed. "Mommy, don't cry."

"I'm fine, honey. Don't you worry. You go home with your daddy tonight. I'll see you tomorrow."

"Come on, Jere. Let's let your mom rest," and he took the girl by the hand. He cast a parting glance at Stephanie as they left the room. She lay motionless, eyes closed, tears wetting the sides of her face. He held himself back from returning to her side to gently stroke her hair, her hand, her face. He knew she'd be all business again in a week or two, and a dull depression descended on him. With that thought he stopped short and turned back. "Stephanie, how…?"

"Your little friend - Juana Salcedo."

He turned and left the room, fearful of Juana's fate after her heroic sacrifice to save his wife and daughter. Ex-wife, he reminded himself.

***

He'd been sleeping fitfully when Francesca found him and Jere on the couch. The housekeeper hadn't heard them enter, and didn't expect them for another three days, but one look at Ben's face kept her questions in check.

"Stephanie's been hurt. She'll be here later today. Take care of her, will you? I'll be back later. And Francesca," he added, looking at the older woman with a seriousness she'd rarely seen, "we are in a code red here. No one comes in. Keep the phone on you. Jere does not go out. I'll have the police do drive-bys as often as they can."

"Si, Senor," Francesca lapsed into her native tongue, Ben's gravity striking fear in her.

"Let Jere sleep as much as possible. She's been through a terrible ordeal. Don't leave her alone," he added as he arranged the blanket snugly around the sleeping girl.

"Si, Senor."

Forced to drive his pickup, he made a mental note to locate the bike. He'd have to reassemble it, but it would give him a chance to make some changes he had in mind. The turbo and brakes needed adjusting. He probably should put on a new set of tires while he was at it too. Working on the bike helped calm him and provided temporary respite from the pounding anger and anxiety he often felt. It was an alternative to boxing, anyway.

Unmindful of the traffic, he drove with his thoughts completely focused on the case at hand. Where did the Cactus Murders end and the findings of the task force merge? Were the events that occurred in Cabo the direct result of that melding? Too tired to think clearly, he hoped the day wouldn't be wasted. He needed to think clearly and to see the connections he felt were staring him down.

He arrived at the cafeteria twenty minutes early, obtained a large cup of double espresso mixed with some other expensive Italian-sounding ingredient, and waited for the fog in his brain to dissipate. Notebook out, he wrote down names that teased him: Michael Lorenzo (aka Miguel Lorenzo); Vincente Basilli; Bill Passkey; and suddenly Hiro Matsuya's name appeared on the tablet.

The scraping of Chloe's chair disrupted his train of thought.

"Good morning, Chloe. Thanks for meeting with me. And thanks for coming to the rescue down there. I never did thank you last night. I…"

"That's what the posse does, Ben."

He didn't know how to express the gratitude he felt. Thank you just didn't seem adequate.

"Chloe, I…I've been kind of an ass about you and Mack. You don't deserve that, especially after all you've done for me and…"

"We're even, okay? That's what friends are for, and besides you pay me well." He could see that she was trying to keep things light. He'd oblige, but he still felt like a jerk.

"Let's get started then," he said as he finished his espresso and raised the cup to the barista to order another. "You first. Tell me about the Brunkee girl."

"Well, you were right. She's Starr's step-daughter. Her death was very unexpected and suspicious. On the surface it looks like she was a totally non-drug using kid, then used once with fateful consequences. Starr hushed things up to protect his wife – and probably his career. No crime in that really. She's buried on the property in the family plot like you thought she might be. I can't see any crime in the cover-up. People do it all the time…people with influence anyway. It might've been a bad decision on his part, but the scandal could've cost him his job. Certainly his credibility."

"So, what're you thinking?"

"I'm thinking she used once and had heart failure. It's not unheard of."

"Any suspects at all?"

"No. The girl wasn't even dating anyone that I could find out."

"So, is Starr the Cactus Murderer? What's your gut feeling on that?"

"I hate to say it, but I think he could be. He certainly has motive, and he has opportunity. But there's no proof whatsoever. A million people out there have motive and opportunity. If it wasn't for his daughter's death, he wouldn't even be on the radar at all. I think it's shaky, Ben. Plus, think about his coming down to help you. If he were guilty would he come riding in on the white horse to save his accuser?"

"Maybe he was coming in to save Stephanie. Did you think about that?"

"Yes. I did. I don't think so though. He's devoted to his wife who, it turns out, fell off her horse a short time after the daughter's death and has been a paraplegic ever since."

"I'm not sure I could bring him down after his help yesterday anyway. Don't dig any deeper. I don't want to know. I'm scratching him off my suspect list of one."

"I understand," she said simply. He knew she wasn't in complete agreement with his decision, but mercifully she didn't criticize or argue.

"So what now?" she asked.

"Okay. I was compiling names that have been nagging at me. I have Lorenzo, Passkey, Basilli and…ready? Matsuya?"

"Matsuya from Juneau? Shipping magnate Matsuya?"

"Yeah."

"What makes him pop up? I agree, by the way on Lorenzo. Something about that guy gives me the creeps. Like his eyes don't match his words. Never heard of Basilli. Never want to hear of Passkey again."

"Well, Matsuya has the ships and the obvious drug connections, and he's an enterprising guy, let's face it. He walked on the Juneau bust."

"What brings up the shipping connection? When did this enter the picture?"

"I think there's something there, Chloe. I can't explain it though, but I'm hoping that Starr levels with me about the goddamn task force. Maybe that'll make a connection. They're onto something and I'm out of the loop. Out of the loop to the point where my wife, ex-wife," he quickly corrected himself, "and daughter were in jeopardy. Instead, I'm thrown off everything with this Betsy Brunkee bullshit. I feel like I'm in a goddamn maze." His agitation forced a few surrounding people to eye him uneasily.

"Ben, go back to what you do best. Your crazy charts and graphs. Have you charted this? Done your diagram magic or whatever it is you do?"

"No, I haven't. It's a stupid waste of time."

"Maybe you should. You're right about the intentional confusion. Maybe we should take each name and systematically go to the books."

"I don't have the time, Chloe. Then there's Juana Salcedo too."

"How does she fit in?"

"Stephanie told me last night it was Juana who got her and Jere freed. I don't even want to think about what might've happened to her if Passkey got his hands on her."

Chloe remained silent, and he could see he was overwhelming her with his moody brooding. He needed to take action. He needed to follow her advice. Starr had to level with him so he at least had a full deck of cards to assemble. As it was he felt like he was trying to bat with a blindfold on.

"Listen, Chloe, you don't have to stay on this case. You've done more than enough."

"Damn you, Ben. You bring Bill Passkey into it and you expect me to just la-ti-da walk away like nothing's happened?"

"Sorry. I just know he's involved in more than the kidnapping of my…of Stephanie and Jere. He and Matsuya were the kingpins in the Juneau case. They both walked. I don't think they gave up their pursuit of wealth and happiness for the sake of everyone and everything. Somehow I think they're both involved in a big drug scam again. I think this Basilli is a Middle-East connection. He makes a respectable Italian, but there are slip-ups. He's Arab, and I'd bet my next paycheck on it."

"So, let me get this straight. You think Passkey and Matsuya are shipping drugs. You think Basilli is a Middle-East connection. And Lorenzo?"

"I think that bastard is the Mexican connection. I think he's playing both ends. He's in a perfect position to do so. Think about it. He's privy to the task force information. He used to work for Starr in the damn U.S. Marshal's office, for crying out loud. Yet he keeps a villa or whatever in Mexico and lives there as much as he does here."

"You want I should check him out? Do a little sleuth job?"

He could tell she wanted him to laugh, but he persisted in his intensity. "No. You've done enough already."

"Ben, I'm leaving April 19th. I'm available until then. I don't want to sit around and twiddle my thumbs. Let me help."

"Listen, I gotta go meet Starr. Why don't you come along and see if you can sit in the meeting. He may ask you to leave. If so, I'll call you later, and if I have a job for you, I'll let you know."

"Okay. Let's go then."

The elevator crawled, stopping on almost every floor before they entered the foyer of the U.S. Marshal's Office. It was exactly 10:00 a.m. when they emerged from the stuffy elevator, Ben's caffeine rush now fully upon him. Starr stood in the lobby, closing a cell phone.

"Just tried to call you. You look like crap, by the way. You get any sleep last night?"

"About four hours."

"How's Stephanie this morning?"

Ben stood silent. What a shithead. He hadn't even called to check on her. "She's fine. Doing well. She'll be discharged today."

"Well, we'll be done in time so you can probably go pick her up. Your bike's at my place, by the way. Bud dropped it off early this morning. It's in a lot of parts, gotta warn you. He had to disassemble it more to get it off the plane by himself."

"I got my pickup. No problem. I'll swing by and get it later this week."

"Good. Let's go in the office and get started. No calls, Janet," he informed his secretary, who nodded affirmatively.

The three entered Starr's large, sterile looking office. It was the antithesis of the magnificent work space Ben had seen in his home. This room was austere and plain, with bold white walls and cheap furnishings. No wonder he worked at home so much, Ben mused.

"Have a seat and make yourselves comfortable. Need coffee? Tea? Water's on the table, so help yourself." He sat down with a yellow legal pad before him.

Ben waited for the barbed questions regarding the Betsy Brunkee affair, but Starr began the meeting with an overview of the Task Force's area of concentration – the illegal shipping of narcotics from Mexico into the United States.

Chapter Twenty

"HERE'S where we are," Starr began "We know already that the U.S. Mexican border is as porous as a sieve when it comes to drug trafficking. We've got people like Martinez-Gomez behind bars who have convinced even the most obdurate in Homeland Security and DEA that the drug trafficking in this country is completely beyond control."

Refresh me," Ben said.

"Martinez-Gomez was the guy supplying meth to the Midwest, mostly Minnesota and North Dakota. The cartel that ran him is in Sinaloa where they produce an especially addictive form of meth, then ship stockpiles here. Gomez was just one of several suppliers, but he alone was taking $250,000 a month for his cut."

"You wouldn't think of the Midwest, especially someplace like North Dakota, as being a big drug use area," Chloe commented.

"You ain't seen the half of it. Everybody thought drug use might fall once ephedrine was taken off the drug store shelves. That only shut down the mom'n'pop operations and basically paved the way for people like Martinez-Gomez. My friends in DEA tell me that Mexican cartels now control at least 80 percent of the meth sold in the central part of the U.S. Their business costs Minnesota, for example, hundreds of millions of dollars a year. All of this is coming over the border. If they send ten cars carrying the shit and two get caught, it doesn't matter to them because eight get through. There are major distributors all over the United States. Denver, Seattle, Boise. You name it."

"So, the border leaks. Tell me something new," Ben said.

"It's not just the Texas, New Mexico, Arizona, and California borders, Ben. We know it's coming in on ships too. Our first big insight into how much was the Jose Tejita Valencia Cruz case. He shipped tons of shit here from Columbia. His was probably one of the biggest U.S. drug investigations ever. His little ring probably made two billion dollars in the '80s, shipping over one hundred tons of cocaine."

"So what the hell's being done about it?"

"Unfortunately, since 9/11 most of the attention on shipping is being focused on keeping radioactive and nuclear material out. We're busy running around signing agreements with everyone, even countries like Jamaica. The Container Security Initiative, CSI, works to team people from the U.S. Customs and Border Protection and the Immigration and Customs Enforcement to target and to prescreen containers destined for the U.S. The CSI is only operational in 44 ports worldwide, and the United States' maritime borders include 95,000 miles of open shoreline. There are 361 ports along this country's expanse of shoreline, and basically the U.S. relies on ocean transportation for 95% of cargo tonnage that moves in and out of the country."

"Who keeps track of all of this shipping traffic?" Chloe asked, looking stunned by the information.

"The United States Coast Guard has primary responsibility for most of it. Federal law authorizes the Coast Guard to board vessels, make inspections, searches, seizures and arrests. They also are authorized to regulate the handling of dangerous cargos at waterfront facilities. Their responsibility is vast and, I believe, quite overwhelming. Each Coast Guard Captain of the Port can employ any security measures deemed necessary to ensure the safety and security of the port he's assigned. This, mind you, is in addition to protecting life and property at sea, protecting the marine environment, maintaining buoys, breaking ice, and I'm sure a dozen other things I've forgotten about."

"So, let me get this straight. You know the border leaks drugs, and…"

"No, Ben. The border pours drugs - as in a torrential flood."

"Okay. Pours drugs. We apparently can't stop that for whatever reasons, and now you're thinking they're coming by sea also?"

"The task force looked carefully at this idea. We know it's happening, but we don't know where or how. The Coast Guard now requires a 96 hour notice by any vessel before its arrival in the United States. They demand a list of everybody on board with all their identification – like date of birth, nationality, passport numbers, etc. Plus the ship has to identify its vessel name, point of origin, registered owner, etc. They have 96 hours to sort through this information on every single ship that approaches. Remember there are hundreds of ports along the U.S. coast line. Every year there are more than 7500 commercial vessels that make approximately 51,000 port calls. Over six million marine containers enter into the United States every year. And, like I said, so far the emphasis has been on preventing nuclear and radioactive materials from entering the country.

"We've studied the records in minute detail. We can't see where it's happening."

"Is it possible that some ships don't check in? Maybe they just anchor and send things ashore in a row-boat or whatever you call the small boats they carry," Chloe commented.

Starr laughed. "You're right. I'm sure there are ships that set anchor or enter smaller ports without clearance. They could transport merchandise in their 'tenders.'"

"Well, what about them?"

"We can only deal with what we can see."

"What makes you think it's coming in on ships anyway?" Ben asked, a memory tugging at him.

"Has to be. It's the growing buzz on the streets. Reliable buzz. We're already seeing a surge in usage. Sometimes I think everybody in the country uses except me…and present company," he responded, trying to make light of his comment.

The three sat silent while the information sank in. Both Ben and Chloe seemed paralyzed with the hopelessness of the situation.

"Well, what the hell are we banging our heads for doing our piddly drug busts? And why does anybody give a shit about the drug carriers being killed in the desert - the good old 'Cactus Murders.' It seems to me like I'm spending a monumental waste of time trying to track down the killer. He's doing us all a favor." Ben trailed off, suddenly remembering that the killer might very well be sitting before him.

"What does Lorenzo know about this?" Chloe asked.

Ben suddenly remembered the quiet guest on the flight north the night before.

"What makes you think he'd know something?"

"Well, he *is* Mexican…"

Starr smiled. "Be careful with your racial profiling there, Missy, so is half the population of Phoenix."

"Point well taken," Ben said. "But the fact is, he gave Stephanie the information on Betsy Brunkee."

"Did she tell you that?"

"Not exactly. Not in so many words."

"Let's not get side-tracked here. We'll deal with Lorenzo and Betsy Brunkee at another time."

"So – you are telling us this for…?"

"Ideas, Ben. You were in on the Juneau bust of Bill Passkey and Hiro Matsuya."

"Some bust. They both got away."

"Still, tell me what you know about Matsuya."

"Well, let's see, he has a small shipping line. About five ships as I recall. He was running drugs into Juneau. His girlfriend pretended to be a 'buyer' of Oriental artifacts and was shipping them back to the area. The drugs were either in the pieces or used as packing. No one really suspected her because her husband, ex-husband when I came on the scene, was the D.A. in Juneau."

"Tell me about Bill Passkey."

"Low life of all low lifes. Dirty DEA. Basically responsible for Chloe's forced retirement. Murdered or maimed almost everyone he came into contact with. Undoubtedly has a vendetta against me since I spoiled his Juneau caper."

"Which would explain then why he went after Stephanie and Jere."

"Exactly."

"Which will be the reason why he comes after you here."

"There's someone else that needs looking at," Ben offered. "A guy named Vincente Basilli. I know him from somewhere, but I can't place it. I'm sure he's Arab, although he does a good job of passing himself off as Italian."

"And why should we be interested in him?"

"Just a feeling. He was in Cabo. I just think he knows Passkey. I think I've seen him before, but I can't place it. I think I remember Stephanie mentioning the name."

"In point of fact, his name came up in the last task force meeting. We think he could be a serious player in the drug trade. I'll move him to the front burner and get someone checking him out. Anything else?"

"Yes. Juana Salcedo. See if she can be located. She's the one who got Stephanie and Jere free. She has a sad history with Passkey. I'm worried he may take his anger out on her."

"I'll do what I can."

"Get her into the states if you can. She deserves it."

"Like I said, Ben, I'll do what I can." Starr paused. "I'm all ears if you've got any ideas."

Ben hesitated. He remembered the tender running back and forth between the cruise ship and someplace ashore. He vaguely recalled Juana mentioning Passkey and drugs on ships when she'd come to tell him about Stephanie's abduction…Was it worth mentioning? Maybe it would lead on a wild goose chase, but…

"You're going to say something, Ben?"

"Well," he stalled. "I did notice something that struck me as odd at the time. There was a cruise ship anchored offshore, and…" he continued the story, gathering confidence in the possibility even as he spoke. He could see that Starr and Chloe were intrigued by the thought of the drugs finding their way to the states aboard cruise ships.

"How would they be getting the drugs aboard without being seen by passengers? Some people stay aboard," Chloe said.

"You're right. But what if they were pumping it into a holding tank or some container on the ship. They could be actually unloading small barrels or boxes of the stuff. Maybe make it look like food supplies or something," he suggested, becoming excited about the possibilities of his observation.

"Don't these ships get checked by the Coast Guard when they come into harbor?" Chloe asked.

"I'm assuming at this point that they would," Starr said. "I know customs and immigration would be checking people. How closely the ship itself is checked, however, is anybody's guess at this time. I'm sure the Coast Guard considers the cruise ships a low priority for risk."

"But they may not be," Ben said almost inaudibly. "Think about the terrorists who might sneak board. I know they check papers when people return to the ship, but someone could use forged documents. It's not like it's never been done."

"Customs and Immigration would probably detect any stowaways trying to get in illegally. But as for the ship itself?" Starr pondered aloud.

"They could carry the drugs in a hold. Say, a water tank or something. Who would check there?" Chloe asked.

"Anybody feel like taking a little Mexican cruise with me?" A small smile briefly visited Starr's stern face.

"They'd never do it with someone like you on board. If they're using cruise ships, they probably check passenger lists themselves to make sure that snoopy people like the likes of us aren't around." Ben's comment was undeniably true.

"All right. Let's all sleep on this idea and see where we go. Meanwhile, I'm going to alert our Coast Guard friends to the 'possibility' of cruise ships carrying drugs. It should be easy enough to find out which one was in Cabo two days ago and do a check it out thing when the ship comes back to port."

Ben assumed the meeting was drawing to a close, but Starr halted him with an upheld hand.

"Got one other tidbit for you."

"There's more? Not sure I can take any more doom and gloom," Ben tried to say good-naturedly.

"The airlines. Lorenzo slipped up big and mentioned to the pilot about shit coming in on commercial flights. You get any whiff of this?"

"No, but it seems completely reasonable and doable now that I'm hearing about it."

"I'm going in to meet a 4:20 flight from San Jose del Cabo this afternoon. If you have time, join me."

"What makes you think it'll be on that flight?"

"Greed. If the airlifts are working, they probably have a load on every flight."

"I do have one question," Ben hesitated, his demeanor changing. "Where's Lorenzo? Maybe he knows more than we give him credit for.

Lorenzo was indisposed this morning. I'll be talking with him this afternoon," Starr stated flatly, rising and indicating that the meeting was over.

"I'd sure like to be there," Ben's tone was more forceful than he intended.

"You should probably go get Stephanie. I believe she's being released in at noon," Starr responded flatly

How would he know that, Ben wondered, unless he called.

"One last thing," the marshal added. "I'm going to place someone outside your home for a while. Just to make sure your friend from Cabo doesn't make any unexpected house calls while you're at work."

"Thank you," Ben replied, holding his accusatory thoughts in check. He wanted so much to ask about Betsy Brunkee, but after Starr's offer of protection he felt like an ass for even thinking of bringing the subject up.

Chapter Twenty-One

MIGUEL Lorenzo's bloody, swollen, battered hands ached and throbbed painfully. He'd pounded in vain for hours on the log walls. He was starving too. Starr had stuck him in the log shed upon their arrival from the airstrip, securing the heavy door with at least two padlocks and a 2 x 4 placed horizontally across the entry, secured by steel brackets. He knew it was pointless to yell but still he bellowed occasionally. No passersby would ever be around the ranch, and any ranch hands would stay well away if commanded to do so by Starr.

"I have to get my story straight," he told himself for the umpteenth time as he rapidly paced. "Get my story and stick with it. Don't change. Maybe confess to a few little things – it'll make me look more truthful."

Okay. What would the story be? Depended on what Starr asked. He needed to prepare several stories, like back-ups.

He made a mental list and decided he could give up the airline connection if necessary. That was Passkey's baby anyway, and Passkey probably already had a contract on him because of the kidnapping fiasco, so what the hell. Maybe, if he was lucky, Passkey was dead already. That was good. He could negotiate with the airline business. That would appease Starr and maybe get him off the hook for the folder on Betsy Brunkee.

Why had he given the folder to the lawyer woman anyway? Starr would want to know. "Okay. That's the story I gotta work on. Why, oh why, would I give that info. to that woman?" He needed a line to think clearly. He couldn't think in this sweltering log box, and he kicked violently at the wall, instantly grimacing and limping to a corner away from the door where he slid to the floor.

"I gave the folder to the woman because…" and his vacant mind stalled. "I gave it to her because – because – because I…" His mind blanked. The truth was he wanted to impress the tall, willowy, extremely charming woman. He delighted in dreams of snatching her out from under Starr and the ex. This juicy morsel would disparage Starr so that he'd lose all possible credibility and respect with her. He knew she'd pass the information on to her ex who would put Starr on his list of Cactus Murder suspects. He himself suspected Starr of the savage murders. The man certainly had motive after the death of the daughter and subsequent devastating accident of the wife's. So, how could he tell this to Starr? He couldn't. He'd have to make up some poppycock or other.

He had all day – or at least until Starr returned. So, what kind of bullshit could he come up with? Ah! He had it! He was being blackmailed into giving the information out. "That's it! Someone was blackmailing me. Someone who wants to discredit you, Jake. Someone who wants your job, man! They threatened me. Threatened to turn me over to the cartels for ratting them out."

Ah, this was getting good. But, how would that person have known? "How the fuck do I know? Information gets out. Maybe the medical examiner said something. How do I know? I just know I was being blackmailed, man!"

He felt instantly better. Yahoo! He had the airline story for trade and a good blackmail story for survival going. Still, he had to be careful. Starr would trip him up if he wasn't sharp. On his toes. He began to feel better. If he could just eat though, but he knew that food deprivation was a method for getting people to talk. They got weak and easily confused.

"Okay, I got my story. I'm good to go. I don't say nothin' about the girl. Mum's the word. He's got no clue. I'm good. I'm almost home free." The thought of Passkey shot through his head, but he could only deal with the devil before him right now. He'd kill Passkey if he had too, if the man wasn't dead already.

"Damn cell phones never work when you want 'em to," he murmured as he leaned over to pick up the two pieces that had flown off the dead phone when he'd hurled it across the room. "I'm gonna carry a spare after this is over. Never gonna be caught without a phone again, goddamn it!"

Exhaustion finally overtook him as he lay down on the floor and closed his eyes.

***

Starr had enormous manpower at his disposal, and he used it all, Thanksgiving break or not. Assistants were called in and directed to work on the cruise ship lines and their schedules. He had Janet get Mathew Johnson, someone on the upper rungs of the Coast Guard career ladder, on the phone for him.

By noon he knew there were at least seventeen major cruise lines, each with at least a dozen ships, most more. Locating the cruise lines sailing to Mexico was not difficult, however, and a few calls later he knew the ship Ben had seen in Cabo San Lucas two days earlier was, aptly, one of the Fiesta Cruise Lines ships. It was due back to Los Angeles in four days. He wanted someone there.

He had his harried secretary send faxes and e-mails to the major players in Washington and California. His reputation was the only card he had to play to convince his fellow law enforcement comrades to heed his idea. He hoped Ben was right about his hunch and that this was not a monumental waste of time.

Cruise ships were inspected carefully for health violations since outbreaks of gastrointestinal disorders left scores of people ill, some even hospitalized. Air, food, and water samples were taken regularly. But waste water, sewage, and garbage would not be inspected, probably ever, by anyone, he came to learn. The magnitude of that omission was mind-blowing, almost impossible to comprehend.

The disposal of sewage was a huge fiasco. In the past, ships had dumped sewage offshore, but environmentalists and health officials had finally convinced most American ports to accommodate the pumping of bilge effluent into sewage tanks ashore. He knew there were several congressional bills floating around, mostly in the Pacific Northwest, limiting the dumping of sewage and "gray water." It would make sense that a ship could discharge a lot of narcotics under the guise of sewage disposal. If the ships could carry tens of thousands of gallons of sewage, who would notice if a couple of thousand gallons of sewage space was diverted for another use.

He'd take a handful of his crew to work the tip Lorenzo had unwittingly given Lewinski about using commercial airlines to smuggle drugs. The airlines were checked regularly, so it was pretty improbable that they could stash a suitcase or two, or a box or two of narcotics aboard a plane. Since food service was all but nil, that eliminated another possible smuggling situation. Hell, maybe it's in the sewage onboard the planes too, Starr thought.

"This will be a day that could make or break my career, Janet," he said cheerily to his secretary as he left for the airport, deputies in tow. He was, in some respects, beyond the call of his official duties with this drug case, but the U.S. Marshal's Office was the oldest and most versatile federal law enforcement agency there was. He didn't want to stop and think about it.

He normally was a fugitive hunter, not a drug-buster, but since the death of his daughter, his involvement in the drug world had taken precedence. He smoothed over his superiors' possible objections by referring frequently to the notorious "Cactus Murders." No one said much. Jake Starr was a well-liked and respected lawman.

At the last minute Ben arrived. "Sorry. Traffic was a bitch."

"Not to worry. I'll fill you in on the way. Chloe joining us?"

"No. I didn't ask her to."

"How's Stephanie?"

"Better. Traumatized. Her legs and feet are swollen, but the doctors seemed to think a few days of carefully applying periodic ice packs and rest would probably take care of it. There may be some nerve damage. Too soon to tell."

"How's your kid?"

"Pretty bad, emotionally. Very clingy. Terrified."

"Sorry to hear that," Starr said, changing tone and gears, "By the way, did you clear this with your department?"

"I'm still on vacation."

"Okay. Let me introduce you to the crew today."

Introductions made, the group rode in a no-siren van to Sky Harbor Airport, disembarking at the airline gates that serviced Cabo San Lucas.

"Let's divide and conquer, men. The dogs and their handlers will have their arrival times staggered. I don't want to set off any alarms. Each group will be escorted by airport security to baggage and maintenance. Make sure the dogs get a whiff of the sewage. I want them on the planes before anything is taken off or cleaning crews allowed on. This is a potential combat situation. You all got radios. Talk to me. Don't anybody try to be the Lone Ranger here."

Serious faces nodded agreement. Bill Passkey's grand plan was about to crash land.

***

Passkey lay dormant in the Mexican hospital. Barely alive from loss of blood by the time he arrived unconscious in the Red Cross ambulance, his condition was marginal. Unable to attach his appendages, since no one had brought them along and they were not to be found when the police went to retrieve them, doctors scratched their heads in uncertainty and consternation. The man would probably die. If he survived?

"I doubt he'll survive. Best to spend your time with other patients," the staff was instructed. "His blood tests came back HIV positive anyway. At least he won't be spreading it around anymore."

Even as he lay almost dead, the forces of evil were conspiring within him to wreak havoc on those who'd betrayed him, and the list was long. By morning he'd be conscious enough to form a hit list. The thought of the death directory alone was enough to sustain life in the traumatized, mutilated man. Juana Salcedo and Benjamin Thomas topped the register. Miguel Lorenzo figured prominently, and what the hell, he'd take out Vincenti Basilli also. He'd kill every bastard whore who worked for him, and then he'd cut the doctor's dick off and see if he didn't have a change of therapy in mind. Anger revived him. He'd demand some blood, not Mex blood, and get the hell out of the place. He'd rest at home. Hire someone to take care of him. Pills. He needed pills. Dull the pain, get some blood, and he'd be good as new. How the hell was he going to take a piss?

He lay cursing and crying. "Yes. I'll kill them all."

The medical staff huddled outside his door, drawing straws to see who'd have to enter the room to deal with the ranting maniac.

Chapter Twenty-Two

JAKE Starr sat in his study, a full tumbler of whiskey in his hand. He couldn't move. He couldn't think. He only stared at the glass as it shattered in his vise of a grip. A whoosh of air escaped, as though he'd been struck in the solar plexus with a battering ram. Rage and grief vied for dominance. Both would have to be appeased, he knew. He gave in without a struggle and let the rage swell and roil. A hot flush flooded his stomach while blood pounded in his head. He knew he'd kill him. He'd kill him, stomp him, murder him and enjoy every second.

He pulled his Glock from its holster but decided against it. He'd use the .44 magnum. He'd blow a hole through the slimy, pile-of-shit bastard. He'd drag him into the desert, shoot him, and leave him either to mummify or turn to coyote feed. He didn't care which. While he wanted the man to suffer, he wanted him dead.

"I'll shoot him now. Get it over with. Drag the body out after he's dead," he said to himself as he poured another tumbler of whiskey, wrapping a handkerchief over his cuts from the shards of glass. Shooting Lorenzo though, just didn't seem to equal the magnitude of the loss he had endured. He needed to hack him into pieces – hack his family into shreds. There would never be enough death or suffering to compensate for the loss of Betsy and the resultant devastating accident of his wife.

He returned to the sofa and picked up the long, glorious mane of blonde hair that he'd found in Lorenzo's dresser in the traitor's

Scottsdale condominium. There was no question who the golden locks belonged to. He'd stood paralyzed when he saw the foot long bundle secured by ribbon. Unable to speak, barely able to move, he'd staggered to his car holding the ponytail to his chest with one hand, the other hand out for balance, not caring about the drug related evidence he'd gone in search of.

Nor did he remember the long drive to his ranch; he only knew by the bile in his throat that he'd heaved everything from his stomach somewhere along the stretch of I-10.

His hand shook as he raised a newly filled glass to his lips. He should've seen the warning signs. Now he recalled Lorenzo being present, mewling around under some phony pretext, every time he turned around. With glorious hindsight he realized that Lorenzo's glances at Betsy had spoken volumes. How could he have been so deaf to their intent? He pounded his head as he felt another wave of heaving roll through his stomach.

What should've been a red letter day for him had turned into a black day of mourning.

He took the .44 from the glass gun display case in his office and loaded it. He'd drag him into the desert and shoot him there. No mess to clean up – only the slug to retrieve and the gun to re-oil. It was after midnight. He needed to move on this now. Two hours into the desert – two back. He'd easily be at work by 9:00, certainly by 10:00.

He changed quickly, exiting the silent house and walking through the cool night air to the stable. The ancient groomsman, Poncho, greeted him as he entered but said nothing further when he saw Starr's face. The stable hand merely nodded respectfully and retreated to his adjoining rooms. Starr knew no words were necessary, that Poncho understood that his unexpected appearance was related to the yelling man in the shed.

Thirty minutes later, he unlocked the door to the shed and flicked on the lights. He watched Lorenzo startle awake and a look of terror sweep his face.

"This is the end of the trail for you, Lorenzo. Get up. We're going on a short trip."

"Are you going to kill me?"

"Why would I do that, Miguel?" he responded as he quickly and expertly bound the man's hands before he had time to react.

"I don't want to go," Lorenzo whimpered.

"Walk – or be dragged. The choice is yours, but I must warn you, the thorns hurt."

"You're going to kill me like you did the others?"

"What others, Miguel?"

He didn't answer. Instead, "What'd I do, Jake? I done nothing. I just wanted to impress that bitch so I could maybe do her – you know? I didn't mean no harm."

Starr struggled to keep from beating the blithering man to death on the spot. The explosive heat again returned to his head and stomach, and he kicked the prone, quivering man in the side. "Get the fuck up now, or I'll kill you on the spot and spread your filthy body all over the desert!" He paused to regain control. "Go with me, and I'll give you a chance," and he dragged the hysterical man out the door, quickly securing the lasso around him.

"What'd I do, man? You gonna kill me for the stupid report I gave her?" Sobs shook him.

"Report? Oh, that? No, not the report, Miguel."

"What then?" the tethered man screamed as Starr mounted the horse and proceeded to pull him into the dark.

"For this," Starr answered, not turning around but pulling the blonde cascade of hair from under his shirt and holding it up for Miguel to see. "For this."

There was no immediate answer, and Starr turned to double-check that the bastard was still behind him.

"Jake. I can explain. It was an accident, man. A terrible accident! I wanted to tell you, but I couldn't. I – I didn't kill her. Someone else did and gave me the hair to give to you, but I was too afraid, Jake. You gotta believe me, man!" Desperation flooded his voice. "I would never hurt her. I didn't do it! But, I can tell you who did. I was afraid…" his words tumbled helter-skelter. He'd invented so many lies and plausible stories that day that, in his desperation, they became muddled and confused. Which story went with what?

Starr's only response was to put the horse into a slow trot, causing Lorenzo to fall frequently as he pleaded for mercy.

It was not long and there was only the sound of blubbering and praying. Soon after, Jake could tell the man had fallen and was being dragged over the rocky, thorny ground. Good. Pain. An occasional sob broke the otherwise silent procession of the horse through the dark Arizona desert.

Fourteen miles south of his ranch Starr pulled the horse to a halt, dismounted, and walked to the bleeding, prostrate figure on the ground. Most of Lorenzo's skin was worn from his face, torso, and knees. Sand and dirt, mixed with a generous portion of blood, covered the prone, half-conscious captive. Both arms had been pulled from their sockets, another clue Jake knew would be a dead giveaway to an investigator or medical examiner that the man had been dragged. He didn't care.

He dragged the half-dead man to the base of a saguaro, unholstered the .44, and stood before him. He wanted to say something profound, but no words came. Instead, a single shot rang out, blasting the back of Lorenzo's head off, tearing through the base of the saguaro, and burying itself in the hard earth two feet beyond. Acting on experience, he easily located and retrieved the bullet. He would keep it and eventually bury it, along with Betsy's hair, with his wife when she died. He wished the slug could erase his grief and loss the way it had erased Lorenzo.

He spurred the horse towards home.

Poncho said nothing as Starr, drained and weary, returned, handing him the reins of the sweaty animal. "Lost a shoe," he said as he walked sadly away, disappearing into the dark courtyard of the hacienda.

Poncho crossed himself but said nothing to the receding figure, knowing that the desert was now a resting place for the prisoner he'd heard hollering all day.

***

Juana Salcedo stood at the railing, hypnotized by the water hissing along the side of the ferry's hull. It hissed and swished by, little waves streaming out from the boat's wake.

It was quiet onboard. The few deck passengers were huddled in small groups for the night, finding a place to bed down on the hard surface.

She'd made it to La Paz and onto the ferry without capture. But her heart was not as happy as she thought it might be. She felt gratified thinking that Passkey was undoubtedly dead. But it didn't matter. Perhaps it was sweeter revenge if he survived – a eunuch for all time.

She'd given great thought to returning to southern Mexico where her mother had told her she was from. But now she saw no purpose. She knew no one. She knew she was dying of the disease that had no cure. There would be no one to care for her as she wasted away. She'd seen other working girls who'd contracted the strange disease thrown to the streets for dogs to gnaw their bones.

It was better to end things here, tonight, in the beautiful, tranquil sea that seemed to be singing to her with each little swish and wave.

She quickly climbed over the top of the railing and stood on the edge of the ferry, holding on and looking down at the welcoming waters below. Perhaps she would be allowed to swim with the dolphins after she spent her time in purgatory paying for her sin of self-destruction. Or would she sleep forever in the beds of seaweed that covered the bottom of the sea?

She removed one hand from the railing, hesitated, then re-grabbed it. She knew she was committing a mortal sin by taking her own life. A terrible sin. But was it any worse than any of the other stains she'd incurred on her soul?

She felt profoundly tired, and weak. It would be so easy to let go and drop into the calming water. She remembered floating in the water outside of Passkey's house. She'd felt so peaceful with the stars looking down upon her.

She let go, crossed herself, and prayed for forgiveness as she disappeared into the black waters.

Her small bag of belongings sat beside the railing. In the morning a deckhand moved the bag aside. An old lady said she remembered seeing a young woman with the bag, so when no one claimed it the bag went, as though by default, to the old crone.

***

Ben fought the almost unbearable urge to call Starr the next day after the airline raid. He wanted to rehash Starr's brilliant success at the airport, but out of deference to Stephanie he denied himself the impulsive desire to speed down to the Gila Bend ranch or to call.

It was good having Stephanie in the house, and she seemed more amiable than he'd anticipated given that he assumed she must be blaming him for her and Jere's kidnapping. She smiled warmly when he entered whatever room she and Jere were in. The little girl clung to her mother, and Ben dreaded the scene which would have to play out when Stephanie prepared to leave for her own home.

"How are you feeling?" he finally asked that afternoon when she left Jere asleep on the bed where they'd been reading and re-reading the girl's childhood books.

"I'm doing fine, Ben," she answered as she hobbled on crutches. "Let's sit on the porch, shall we? It's so nice out – not too hot."

"Sure. You want some iced tea or anything?"

"Tea would be nice, thank you."

Moments later Francesca arrived carrying a tray with tea and a small platter of fruit. Ben smiled. "You forgot the chips and salsa, Francesca."

"No chips and salsa, Senor. Fruit is better for Senora Stephanie."

"You have a nice home here, Ben," Stephanie commented after a few moments of silence.

"Well, I'm not much about the decorating part, but I like the house. I should probably hire an interior decorator or whatever to fix it up better."

"It's nice. It's a nice home for Jere."

"Yeah. Close to school. Pretty safe community."

He sensed that the small talk was as hard for Stephanie as it was for him. Suddenly, it was out in the open.

"Ben, I want to talk with you about something." She paused, and he remained silent. "I guess I want to tell you how much I enjoyed our vacation together in Mexico, that is until…you know."

"Yeah. I really know how to show a girl a good time."

"Nonsense. That was not your fault."

"It was, Stephanie. You're right. My job jeopardizes Jere – and you. I plan on quitting the department after I finish up one more thing."

"Forget about the Cactus Murder assignment, Ben. Quit now, for god's sake, while you're still whole and alive!"

"It's not the Cactus Murder job, Stephanie."

Her eyes widened. "No! Please, please let this kidnapping thing go. Please!"

"What kind of a man would I be if I let this asshole who threatened my wife," he paused to try to correct himself, "you, and Jere get away with it?"

"You'd be a smart man, for god's sake! Just start over, Ben. Start all over. Let's go back to the beginning."

"What are you talking about? The beginning of what?" He wouldn't make this easy for her; she hadn't made the last seven years of his life easy. He watched her face carefully and saw such sadness sweep over it that it was all he could do not to recant his words.

"Ben, I made a terrible mistake when I left you and Jere. I know it now. I've known it for years, but I've been too proud to come before you and beg forgiveness. Before I beg, is there a chance? At all?"

He drew a deep breath. Here he'd thought the trip was about her wanting custody of Jere.

"What is it you want, Stephanie. Be honest with me. No more games."

"I'd like to see you – more. I'd like to see if we can work things out, somehow. I know I've made a terrible mess of things. I didn't deserve you, Ben, and I don't deserve your love now, but…"

He paused. "I don't know what to say."

"You don't have to say anything now. Please, just think about it. I'll understand if you don't want to give it another try."

"I just don't know what to say," he said again.

"Just tell me you'll leave the department and walk away from this mess – you can say that for starters."

It came crashing down on him as he sat there. Was she going to try to run his life again? "Stephanie, there's one thing you need to know up front. I'm NOT going to let this man go. That's a fact and it's not negotiable, so don't say it again. He'll haunt me, you, Jere, the rest of our days if I don't take care of him, do you understand that? Do you want an armed body guard shadowing you for the rest of your life? This mess started in Juneau. It ends here. Once and for all." He stood as though to indicate the conversation was over.

"You're right. I'm sorry. I'm just afraid."

"Stephanie, you'll always live in fear, trust me, if I don't end this and bring him down."

"Why can't someone else do it? Jake Starr's a U.S. Marshal. It's his job to track down fugitives."

"It wasn't Jake Starr's wife and daughter who got kidnapped and terrorized, that's why."

"So you're going to let some guy thing, some big macho idea dictate your actions?"

"Well, I guess it all boils down to the old saying that a man's gotta do what a man's gotta do." He recalled Starr's words as he angrily stalked away. They made perfect sense to him now. He wanted to sit and talk, but he feared the endless banter going in circles. Go or don't go, he thought to himself. Just make a decision and stay with it.

Chapter Twenty-three

THE entire staff heaved a sigh of relief as they watched Bill Passkey wheeled out the hospital doors. No ethical doctor would willingly sign his release, but no doctor was ready to endure the wrath of a terrorized staff.

A taxi delivered the ailing man to his silent hacienda. "Tell all your beaner relatives that I got a lot of job openings here, amigo," he shouted at the departing taxi driver. He hobbled up the few steps to his front door and entered the silent vestibule. A wave of nausea swept over him. Exhausted from his slight efforts, he sank to a settee arranged in the foyer. He knew he needed help. He'd gladly pay to get someone here. He'd call Lorenzo. Lorenzo would help him out. Lorenzo would track down the whereabouts of Ben Thomas for him, but Passkey himself would kill the bastard. He'd save the Mexican bitch that had emasculated him until last. He'd spend every dime he had if necessary to track her down. Already his contacts in Cabo were combing the backstreets and barrios looking for the bitch. He'd get her, sooner or later.

When he awoke the house was dark and his pain constant. "Where the hell are those fucking pills?" he mumbled as he rummaged in his coat pockets. Popping the cap, he swallowed two, then threw in an extra for good measure. "I'll get me some real pain killers soon as I get hold of Lorenzo," he continued to mumble to himself.

After ten minutes, the pain began to subside, and he slowly rose to a bent stance. "Call Lorenzo. Get his ass over here with some help," he reminded himself.

He hugged the wall as he slowly shuffled to his room where he found his cell phone on the nightstand by the bed, but the bloody sheets covered with flies made him gag. He'd sleep on the veranda, he thought as he began pushing numbers on his speed dial. There was a pre-recorded message on Lorenzo's phone which set off a round of cursing and sweating.

He pushed more buttons on his speed dial to no avail. Finally, desperate, he dialed the hospital. "I'll pay someone $10,000 right now, on the spot, and $10,000 a week after that, to come out here and help me," he half-cried, half-bellowed into the phone.

Despite the staff's revulsion, they drew straws to see who would get the prize of $10,000 a week. In the end, for safety's sake, two agreed to share the wealth.

***

Ben spent the better part of the weekend in his garage working on the dismantled Harley. A tinkerer by nature, it was relaxing for him to dismantle, clean, polish, replace and reassemble. Despite his interest in the parts spread before him, he chomped at the bit for Monday's arrival so he could return to work without a guilty conscience about leaving Stephanie and Jere alone. Several times he talked himself into a quick trip to Ajo, but stopped himself each time. He'd see Jake Starr on Monday, slap him heartily on the back, and check on the progress of the operation he hoped would take place when the Fiesta Lines cruise ship returned to port.

Bill Passkey dominated his thoughts also. Technically he didn't need to stay on with the department to exact his revenge. In fact, it was unethical for him to do so. No police department in the world would allow an officer to "get even" no matter the offense. A war waged within him continuously. Should he bring him in and nail his ass for the kidnapping and assault and the Juneau crimes? Would that suffice? Let the justice system do its job? Or should he just erase the vermin?

Mixed in with his murderous ruminations were the thoughts that had visited him in Mexico - thoughts of leaving his career and going in another direction. In Mexico it had seemed easy and comfortable. Back at home it seemed insurmountable. What would he do? How would he support himself and Jere?

As the weekend progressed, he found his mood more and more dour.

"Ben, am I causing a problem for you by being here?" Stephanie asked as he made a small fire Sunday evening.

"A problem? No. What makes you say that?"

"You just seem so remote since our last conversation." "Remote?"

"Unapproachable."

"I've got a lot on my mind, Stephanie."

"Want to talk about it?"

He wasn't prepared for her response. In earlier days she'd brushed off his worries and concerns, wanting to focus on them and their relationship instead. He'd learned to leave the problems that plagued him at the station or on the back burner.

"No. Not really."

"Are you going to work tomorrow?"

"Yeah. Vacation's over." He smiled happily, then realized his mistake. "I need to touch base with Starr, and head back to my cubbyhole to check messages, and stuff…" he trailed off.

"I think I'll keep Jere home from school – if that's okay with you."

"Yeah. Probably a good idea."

"Ben, I've been thinking. Maybe, for a while anyway, Jere should stay with me. Until the Passkey thing gets resolved anyway." Her voice was low, and he had to strain to hear her.

"I don't think that's necessary," he said more forcefully than needed. "I've got Francesca, and I can get good local police coverage. I don't think Passkey will track me down here. He'll be looking in Phoenix." She'd committed the capital offense with her suggestion. He'd been right about her intentions after all.

"Just a thought," she responded in a small, resigned voice.

"How long are you staying, anyway? You're welcome to stay as long as you want," he added in a rush. "It would be great for Jere."

"I"ll probably head back to my place tomorrow or Tuesday. I have work to do also," she smiled sadly.

"You can do it here. Use my computer. Or I can go by your place and pick yours up for you."

"No. I feel like I'm out of place here."

"Out of place? What's that mean?"

"I came here hoping we could patch things up. Maybe at least start seeing each other again. You know, test the waters. But you've been so elusive since our talk. I just feel that you're not interested, and if you're not, please tell me." He could see her tears welling again.

"Stephanie – can we talk about this after I take care of a few things? This idea deserves more time and attention than I can give it right now."

"Oh, so you'll put me on your agenda? Your to-do list?"

He could hear anger and petulance creeping into her tone. "It's not like that at all."

“I’m sorry. I’m just so out of line. I’m confused, and scared. I’ll give you all the time you need if you tell me there’s a chance.”

He looked across and saw the beautiful woman he’d once loved – or thought he loved. She was even more beautiful now, if that was possible. She was the mother of his daughter. He’d thought of her every day for the last seven years. His heart had ached for a long time. Why was he putting her off now? He saw her before him, her large brown eyes longing for a sign from him. A morsel of tenderness.

He reached out just to touch her hand, but she grabbed it quickly and brought it to her cheek. Tears ran down her face. He put his arm around her and pulled her gently to him. A lump formed in his throat. “I love you, Stephanie. I always have.” He wanted to tell her he was afraid – afraid of her walking on him again, but the words and sentiments didn’t know how to form. He wasn’t good at this type of thing, he knew it. He stammered, “Yes, I’d like to see how things go.”

***

Jake Starr spent the weekend between his Scottsdale condo and his office, trying not to second guess the repercussions of his actions against Miguel Lorenzo. He knew he’d acted in haste and blind rage, but regret was not his response. Instead, he carefully analyzed his situation. Lorenzo’s corpse could possibly be discovered by Border Patrol. How many people knew Lorenzo had gone with him? Bud, Ben, Chloe, and now Poncho were the names that came to mind. Bud and he went too far back for there ever to be a whisper from him about things. Poncho’s family had been in the Starr household for two generations. That left Chloe and Ben as potential hostile witnesses. They could both be formidable, but would they be? He sighed. Time alone would tell.

He spent most of his time in his office, contacting fellow law enforcement agencies, beginning with the Coast Guard, and alerting them to the possibility that drugs were suspected of being transported aboard the Fiesta Lines. He knew people in high places, and he got their attention despite it being a weekend. He'd go to L.A. on Tuesday and observe the operation if it could be assembled that quickly. It was asking a lot of agencies to act immediately, with a minimum of evidence. No evidence, really, if it came right down to it. Just good cop hunches.

He'd take Ben along. He deserved to go. The credit would go to him. He'd see to it. He half expected to hear from Ben over the weekend, and was surprised when he didn't. He'd have to deal with him sooner or later over the Passkey issue. Ben would want his revenge, and who was he to deny him? But how involved could he get? As a U.S. Marshal, tracking fugitives was a large part of his job. Granted, he had no jurisdiction in Mexico, but since Passkey was American, he knew he could undoubtedly get authorities there to cooperate, depending on how involved in the drug trafficking they were. No one would turn Passkey over if they were on his payroll or connected, that was for sure.

He made some calls to a few sources in Cabo, and what he learned damn near stupefied him. Dare he tell Ben the man he would be hunting was bed-ridden and half-dead from Ben's little friend putting it to him? There would be minimum resistance - now might be a good time to pay a visit, Starr thought. The man figured prominently on the FBI's list, so snatching him wouldn't raise many eyebrows. Or should he turn a blind eye and let Ben exact his revenge. Did revenge satisfy though? "Too soon to tell," Starr said to himself. Would he be denying Ben satisfaction…or saving him from regret?

He heard the elevator door open and could tell by the footsteps it wasn't Janet. A sharp rap at the door. "Come on in," and Ben's head appeared as he cracked the door open. "Come on in. Just thinking about you."

Ben entered, a seldom-seen smile on his face. "Damn! Good job at the airport, Jake. That was sweet."He smiled in appreciation.

"Thanks. Couldn't'a'done it without some of your input though. Big score for the U.S. Marshal's office, hey?" Quickly he shifted gears, "Let me rustle up some coffee. I make it strong, gotta warn you." He busied himself, wondering how he would break the news to Ben about Passkey, or if he even should.

"You wanna go to L.A. tomorrow? Greet the Fiesta Lines when it comes into port?"

"You got things lined up already?"

"I've been on the phone most of the weekend. I think some of my connections are going to move on this one. Especially after I told them about the bust at the airport."

"Hell, yes, I'd like to go."

"I'll deputize you, how's that?"

"I'm ready now," Ben responded, excitement in his voice.

"You know, Ben, I could really use someone like yourself. You ever think about going to work here?" Starr asked offhandedly.

"Nah. I'm leaving the profession."

"What're you going to do?" He saw him half-heartedly shrug in response. "How're Stephanie and Jere doing, by the way?"

He shrugged again. "Better physically. I think they're both emotionally spent."

"That's understandable, given the circumstances."

"Yeah. Listen, Jake, I really need to get to work. I just wanted to stop by and congratulate you on the bust. It was great! I'll see you tomorrow, though, okay? What time? We flying or driving?"

"Probably take the copter. I'll give you a call this afternoon with the details."

Starr watched Ben leave the office, deciding that he deserved to have his revenge. Revenge had a way of changing a man, but it wasn't just Stephanie and Jere who'd suffered. Chloe was another of Passkey's victims, indirectly maybe, but still… Maybe he'd tell him tomorrow. This was proving to be a tough decision.

Chapter Twenty-four

THE call came, as Ben feared it would, three weeks after the stunning raid of the cruise ship arriving in San Pedro from Acapulco. Jake Starr catapulted overnight to prominence and the law enforcement world clapped vigorously as thousands of pounds of cocaine and meth were hauled from the bilge of the ship. Ben also received accolades, but the praise and media coverage meant little once he knew Bill Passkey lay a day's journey away.

And now the call – the message he dreaded to hear, the message which might force his hand in dealing with the cactus murders. Another body had been found, according to the other agent assigned to the Cactus Murder team he'd been working with."It's a male body, looks to be in his 30's, what we can see of his face anyway. No gray hair. He was dragged for a distance. Some evidence of horse hooves still visible. I'd guess he's been out here better than two weeks…maybe three."

"Okay. I'll be there in a few hours," he sighed.

"This one's different, Ben. The guy was well dressed - before he was dragged. Alligator shoes – what's left of them anyway. Rolex. Remains of a silk shirt. This isn't your usual pack animal."

He sat alert now. "Give me an exact location, will you?"

The detective rattled off the GPS coordinates, then said, "I'll leave a man and vehicle with the body. By the way, this one appears to have been shot – not poisoned. I'd guess a .44 caliber too. The back half of the guy's head has been blown off."

"I'm on my way out the door now." He cradled the phone as he grabbed the paraphernalia he knew from experience that he'd need: camera, hat, sunglasses, charged cell phone, extra clips and a half a dozen bottles of water. He tossed all into a small satchel, along with a pair of old shoes and a small collapsible shovel.

"I'll tell Mayfield you're en route. He'll be on the CB. I can't stay. I gotta be in court this afternoon."

"Roger that." Both men hung up simultaneously.

Do I have everything this time, he wondered as he surveyed the bag's contents.

"I'm outta here, Dina," he called as he exited his office. If she replied, he didn't hear, for his thoughts focused on the absent Miguel Lorenzo. Each time he'd asked Starr about Lorenzo's whereabouts, Starr had smoothly guided him in another direction, never answering, but never seeming to evade.

In their last exchange, Starr had confirmed Ben's worries that Bill Passkey had disappeared, along with two medical personnel. Starr's investigation revealed that an "unknown female assailant" had rendered Passkey a eunuch. It took Ben but a moment to realize that Juana Salcedo had wielded the instrument of revenge. Stephanie's account of her and Jere's rescue left absolutely no doubt.

He involuntarily grimaced as he envisioned Passkey's instruments of torture being severed, but in the next instant he applauded the little Mexican girl. She had more than repaid him. Passkey's unknown whereabouts, however, distracted Ben from the location of Miguel Lorenzo.

Now, as he left the precinct with lights flashing, he suspected he knew where Lorenzo was – a mere fourteen miles from Jake Starr's ranch. Too close for him to ignore.

"Damn it, Jake," he muttered. Despite his growing certainty that Starr was the cactus murderer, he'd let the investigation lapse after the Cabo fiasco. How could he bust the man who basically came galloping in to save his wife, daughter, and probably even himself? "Goddamn it!"

He drove quickly, using Buckeye as far as possible instead of the normally clogged Interstate 10, flashing lights clearing the way. He hoped he was getting ahead of himself. Why would Starr kill the guy so close to his own ranch? It didn't make sense when he really thought about it.

"It could be coincidental," he argued aloud. "Don't get ahead of yourself," he counseled. Enter the crime scene with a clear mind. No preconceived ideas. He knew from experience that many crime scenes were compromised instantly when investigators went in with preconceived ideas, making it impossible to see the scene for what it was. Theories were okay, but only after facts and details were assembled. Details told the tale. Always details.

He brushed Starr from his mind and thought about how he would approach the scene. He decided he'd stop at least fifty yards out and go on foot to the position. Should he alert Starr? No. Leave Starr out of it. What would be the reason to alert him? He realized there were a lot of reasons – one being that Starr had taken Lorenzo to his house when they returned from Cabo and thus might be the last person to have seen him alive; two, the body was found near his ranch. But was the body even Lorenzo's?

The decision was moot, however, when he was informed by Jed Mayfield that U.S. Marshal Starr had already visited the site.

"Did he compromise it in any way?" Ben asked.

"Excuse me, sir?"

"Did he take anything? Move anything?"

"No, sir."

"You watched him the whole time?"

Mayfield stiffened slightly, and Ben took note. "Why are you asking me this, detective?"

"I just want to make certain that the scene is the same as when it was found."

"I'd say it is. Other than some footprints and tire tracks."

"Great." Clearly irritated, he glumly looked around the area. Was it even worth his effort? He took the camera from his satchel and decided he owed Miguel Lorenzo at least a token of his consideration. The man had been shady, conniving, and probably a double agent. For these reasons alone, Ben knew he was well worth the time.

The body had been partially scavenged, but it was still easy to see it was Lorenzo. Despite the early signs of mummification, he could tell by the ligature marks around what remained of his wrists, the tops of the feet, and the general shredding of clothes that the man had been dragged a good distance. Both arms appeared to be dislocated also.

The entry wound of the bullet was clearly visible despite facial decomposition, and judging by the exit wound, the bullet had come from a high caliber weapon – no doubt a .44. Probably a long barrel.

He retrieved his small shovel to excavate the area where the bullet would have lodged upon its exit. Before he even began, however, he saw the earth directly behind the tall saguaro had already been disturbed. The bullet hole's trajectory could easily be traced through the saguaro's base. Someone had beaten him to it.

"You're sure no one touched anything in this vicinity?"

"Not since I've been here."

He dug anyway and, as he suspected, neither the spent bullet nor the shell casing was anywhere to be found. After taking photos, he and Mayfield combed the surrounding one hundred feet. "I don't care what it is. If it's not cactus or dirt, call me," Ben said tersely. The walk around took well over an hour. His soaked shirt clung to him as perspiration streamed down his face. He stopped, disgusted and frustrated. "Go ahead and get him out of here before we get picked off by these vultures. Can you handle everything okay by yourself?"

"Yeah. I got people in the vicinity."

"Okay. I'm heading back." He strode to the car, beginning to feel light-headed, wondering why he'd gone to so much trouble to park so far away. He threw the car door open and started the vehicle without getting inside the 110 degree metal cauldron. He stood, the metal of the vehicle too hot to lean against, and scanned the scorching desert. It was unusually hot for this time of year. It felt more like July than December – or maybe his growing dislike of the human garbage dump the desert had become made him more intolerant.

He was close – he'd stop by Starr's place. Maybe he'd be there.

It was then he noticed something odd looking. It didn't shine or flash. It stuck up at a strange angle amongst the rocks. He almost ignored it, but at the last instant before entering the rapidly cooling vehicle, he walked twenty feet to the rocky area. There was a shoe. A horse shoe.

Chapter Twenty-five

IN seven hours he'd be airborne. He lay in bed, a flood of emotions overwhelming him as he looked about the bedroom. This would be his last day to wake up in the house that he'd hoped would be his forever. He felt sick, and he tried to steer his thoughts away from the nightmare of the last two months and focus instead on the promise of tomorrow when he would sleep in his newly rented flat in London, England. What a kick. London. He supposed he'd have to start drinking tea now.

Next week he would once again be a student – and a teacher. He'd taken the plunge, with much nudging, pushing and shoving from Chloe and Stephanie, and was enrolled in a forensic anthropology program at a school in England. What the hell, maybe strictly investigative work would suit him more than pursuit. Even more interesting, however, was his invitation to do some teaching at Scotland Yard. It was a new chapter for him, and it would start today when he boarded British Airways Flight 7077. All of it was crazy and certainly unexpected.

In the interim, he had only an hour to say goodbye to his house and the life he had hoped to build in it. Things had turned out so badly. His heart began to thump loudly again, pounding mercilessly in his chest, and he slowly sat up and started doing the breathing exercises that helped control the panic attacks that had begun to grip him unexpectedly. He knew that if he focused on his breath, the panic would fade. In time he hoped it would fade forever. Breathe in slowly through the nose to the count of four, he coached himself. Exhale slowly through the mouth to the count of seven. Repeat. Repeat. Repeat. Slowly his heart returned to its normal pattern, and he cautiously arose from the rumpled bed, feeling a small sense of triumph over his autonomic nervous system.

He cringed slightly as he entered the kitchen, avoiding at all cost the bullet sprayed living room that he studiously avoided and had curtained off. He couldn't bear to look at the room where so much tragedy, death and fear had transpired. Blood stained the carpet where Francesca's frail body had fallen in her effort to protect Jere. His long time, sweet, quiet little housekeeper gave her life without a moment's hesitation to save his daughter. He didn't even know her next of kin despite the years of service she'd given him. He buried her in the small graveyard in Wickenburg after a detailed search turned up no relatives in the Las Vegas area.

He stretched his fingers several times after running them under cold water. His hands still swelled and stiffened at night and probably would for some time to come. He'd used them to beat Bill Passkey to death, and he shuddered and gagged as flashes of that horrific night flooded his brain. He still heard the blood spattering as his fists had beat the man senseless. A rage had taken him, a rage that had been building for a long time. Much like a reservoir giving way before a flood, the damage could not be undone. It took three uniformed officers several minutes to pull him off the lifeless body of Passkey. It would take him a lifetime to forget killing the man with his bare hands. The weeks of investigation by his department were almost unbearable and added heavily to the trauma of the whole ordeal.

He tendered his resignation almost immediately after the incident. Despite his superiors' attempts to dissuade him, he knew he couldn't pick up the pieces of his life.

Everything suddenly became so complicated. Answers were so complex and convoluted. He no longer saw things as black and white the way he had for so many years as a cop. Good guy. Bad guy. Criminal. Victim. Instead, he saw a world of multiplying hues of gray.

Thankfully, Jere hadn't witnessed Ben's vicious, brutal beating of Passkey. She'd run from the room, through the kitchen and out the backdoor when Ben swiftly and abruptly entered the room, momentarily distracting Passkey, a split second after he'd opened fire on Francesca. A cop's daughter, Jere knew the 9-1-1 routine as though she'd rehearsed for this moment her entire life.

Passkey had easily tracked him to Wickenburg after the fiasco of Stephanie and Jere's abduction in Cabo San Lucas. Because of the injuries inflicted on him by Juana, however, it took him longer to arrive than Ben anticipated, and so Ben had begun to let his guard relax a bit. Fortunately, his paranoia remained sufficient to maintain in him a state of combativeness despite his outward appearance.

When Jake Starr finally told Ben where Passkey was and what Juana had done to him, Ben's first inclination was to race to Cabo to finish off the toxic cur who spread only poison and despair in his wake. Maybe it was Stephanie, he didn't know, but for some reason he found himself postponing the attack. Plus, no matter how villainous and heinous a person was, Ben couldn't bring himself to attack a man when he was down. He hated this about himself. He wanted to kill Passkey even as the man lay in bed groaning in agony and probably dying, but he couldn't bring himself to do it. Stephanie rallied behind his silent decision to let sleeping dogs lie, but it was an uncomfortable compromise for him. Starr gave him time to reconsider before he went through channels to arrest Passkey, but still Ben hesitated despite his hatred and anger.

"You made the right decision, Ben, whether you know it or not," Starr told him earlier that spring when the two rode through the desert, ostensibly to search for more Cactus Murders which seemed, for no apparent reason, to have stopped.

"So you say. But would you let someone walk who hurt your family? I don't think so."

Starr remained uncharacteristically silent. Finally he spoke, "Ben, revenge isn't all it's made out to be. Trust me, you don't want to know the half of it."

"Like you once said, sometimes a man's just gotta do what a man's gotta do. But what's that say about me?"

"It says you're a better man than I am," and Starr spurred his horse into a lope.

Even now he didn't know the whole story behind Betsy Brunkee and Miguel Lorenzo. He didn't want to know. After the help Starr had given him in Cabo, who was he to sit in judgment on Jake Starr, the best cop he'd ever known?

But now, he frequently reminded himself, it was all academic and behind him. There was only one person left from the Juneau drug bust still on the loose, and that was Hiro Matsuya. He didn't sense that Matsuya was a threat, and he knew he couldn't continue to live his life as though he were. Even Vincente Basilli had disappeared as mysteriously as he'd appeared.

Shower. Shave. He had to be ready by 9:30 for his parents to take him to the airport. They'd insisted, and he didn't want to argue about trifles anymore. They were planning their first visit at the holiday time, and he was glad he'd have company. Stephanie and Jere were also coming. It might even feel like a family again despite the violent unraveling they'd all experienced.

It'd been settled that Stephanie and Jere would join him as soon as possible. He needed time, however, and Stephanie wisely understood that. He'd fallen apart when she and Jere had been abducted, and even though Juana had secured their release before any serious harm was done to them, he couldn't forgive himself for their being taken captive. He hoped, he prayed, that in time he could get beyond the event and pull himself together so that he could offer Stephanie and Jere a life – a good life. Stephanie suggested they stay in Europe indefinitely. She argued persuasively that she could work literally from anywhere in the world thanks to the internet and instant communication. Jere could attend nothing but the best schools. He could do whatever he wanted…or do nothing at all as far as she was concerned. He knew she would take him, for better or worse this time. He couldn't understand why she insisted he was such a good man – a good man does not lose his family.

Despite his best efforts, he could find no trace of Juana. Starr had enlisted the assistance of every Mexican official that he could to help locate the missing woman, but it was as though she had disappeared off the face of the earth. Ben remembered clearly the two dead babies and half-dead girl he'd carried to shade, and he often felt overwhelmed with sadness when he thought of them.

He'd seen Chloe off two days ago, and he'd hugged her with genuine affection and gratitude. Had it not been for her and Starr, Ben knew he would most likely have been killed in Mexico doing something rash in his desperation.

He tried to talk to her, to apologize for the way things had turned out between them, but she would hear none of it.

"Ben, you were right in Juneau. There's always been three of us in this relationship. I tried to deny that. Ignore it. But you were right. None of this is your fault. If anything, you gave me a chance to start over, to build a new life, to finally discover what I really wanted in life. I was so immersed in trying to do the right thing back then. Now I know what the right thing for me really is. I know who the right person for me is, and I have you to thank for all of this." She smiled at him, her eyes teary.

He still couldn't believe that he'd let Mack Jessup walk – how many years ago now? In Craig, he'd been stupefied and dazzled by Chloe. And maybe, deep down, he really hadn't wanted to arrest him. Mack Jessup had been a good excuse for Ben's bad behavior for so long that he'd come to appreciate him.

"Chloe, you take care of yourself. You know I'll be there for you in a heartbeat if you ever need me."

"I know. And I thank you for that."

"Drop me a postcard from time to time, will ya?"

"I will."

A moment later she entered security and he stood alone, watching her as she headed down the long concourse to the gate, never looking back. He felt a lump in his throat and wanted to chase her down. For what? She had Mack waiting for her. She had a new life, and that was what he needed now too – doctor's orders.

"Anybody home?" His mother's voice called at the back door. His leaving would be hard for his parents. They doted on him and Jere. His dad would deeply miss him as a golfing partner, motorcycle riding companion, and friend. His mother, oddly, was ecstatic about his opportunity to live and study in Europe, and was already planning vacations there. Still, he wondered how much was just bravado on her part. They were older now. This was not the best time for him to leave, but she had shushed him instantly when he'd raised these concerns.

"For pete's sake, Ben. You think your father and I didn't have a life before you came along? We'll manage just fine, dear. Not to say we won't miss you, but you need to get on with your life. Maybe we'll sail over and see you. We could deliver your little Nor'Sea 27 to you! Oh! What a splendid idea!" And she'd hurried off to plan a circumnavigation. Since his parents had been blue water sailors in the past, he knew it was not idle chatter on her part. He also knew they would miss him and Jere terribly.

"I'm in the kitchen, mom!"

"You about ready?" she asked as she entered, seeing him still in his skivvies, running cold water on his hands.

"Right on. Ready." And he involuntarily laughed along with her.

"Okay. Just checking on you. We'll be by in about an hour."

"See you then." They both knew she was checking on him because she was worried. He watched her drive away and felt a pang of remorse but brushed it aside for the time being. He could always come back if things didn't work out he told himself as his heart began to hammer again. Breathe in to the count of four. Breathe out to the count of seven. Repeat. Repeat. Repeat. He steadied himself at the sink. He could do this. He would do this. Everything would be okay.

He thought of his brother, Jered, and their last evening together. They'd drunk a few beers and talked about everything but his leaving. Suddenly, however, Jered reached over and patted him on the shoulder. "Hey, everything will be fine, buddy," he said. It was the same pat Jered had given him three decades ago when Ben had dejectedly walked to the dugout after striking out for the umpteenth time. Big brother touches spoke volumes. Ben smiled.

He felt a sudden outpouring of love for his brother. Could he really leave his family behind?

He pictured Stephanie and Jere arriving. Stephanie had already informed him they'd be married again. The thought made him incredibly happy. Meanwhile, he knew Jere would be safe with her. Jake insisted they have a bodyguard until they left the states. Jere needed her mother now. Their ordeal together bonded them in ways Ben could not begin to fathom. His parents would come over...probably on his Nor'Sea 27 if his mother had her way. And he knew his brother, who earned more money than he knew what to do with, would visit with his family also. He wasn't really leaving his family – he was doing his best to get back to them – to be the Ben they once knew.

He felt his pulse slowing and the tension leaving his neck and shoulders. It wouldn't be forever, he counseled himself. Planes flew in both directions. Everything would be fine. He smiled and felt lighter. Everything would be fine.

Author's Note

IN many instances, information in this book concerning the importation of narcotics into this country is accurate. Names of the "guilty" have been changed, but their crimes and the repercussions of those crimes are portrayed as accurately as possible.

The importation and use of narcotics in this country is responsible for the death and suffering of literally thousands of innocent individuals on BOTH sides of the border. No amount of policing will ever be able to stem this flow of drugs as long as there are individuals willing to use these products. Much time and energy is devoted to bringing drug peddlers to "justice." These people would not be a problem in society, however, if there was no market for their product. Perhaps users should be prosecuted with as much ambition and zeal as the entrepreneurs who promote their products. Is it oversimplifying to state that purchasers are the ones who create the market, create the problems and ultimately create misery for so many? Obviously, prosecuting users will never work.

This is the third and final book in the Ben Thomas trilogy. It has been published before the second book in the series because of the timeliness and urgency of the topic.

R.L. Coffield

Titles by Moonlight Mesa Associates, Inc.

Suspense Titles:

Northern Escape. R.L. Coffield. Award-winning suspense. Book I of the Ben Thomas Series. Kindle Edition Available.

Murder in Thomas Bay. R.L. Coffield. Mystery-Thriller. Book II of the Ben Thomas Series. (To be released in 2010)

Death in the Desert. R. L. Coffield. Suspense. International Intrigue. Book III of the Ben Thomas Series. Kindle Edition Available.

Westerns:

Saving Tom Black. A Jake Silver Adventure, Book I. Jere D. James. Kindle Edition Available.

Apache. Book II of the Jake Silver Adventures. Jere D. James. Kindle Edition Available.

Canyon of Death. Book III Jake Silver Adventures. Jere D. James. (Issued in 2011).

The Littlest Wrangler. J.R. Sanders. Young Reader.

Reflections from the Wilderness. Stoney Greywolf Bowers. Cowboy Poetry.

Award-winning Tales from the Corral. Short Story Anthology. (Issued in 2012)

Other Titles:

*Life Was A Cabaret: A Tale of Two Fools, A Boat, and a Big-A** Ocean.* Becky Coffield. Award-winning nonfiction. Kindle Edition Available.

One Pot Galley Gourmet. Becky Coffield. Cookbook.

You Can Conquer TMJ: Ideas and Recipes. Becky Coffield. Cookbook.

Thank you for buying our books. We truly appreciate your interest and support. Visit us on our website:

www.moonlightmesaassociates.com.

Or visit our blog:

www.moonlightmesa.blogspot.com

www.ingramcontent.com/pod-product-compliance
Lightning Source LLC
LaVergne TN
LVHW091046080826
845145LV00002B/645

* 9 7 8 0 9 7 7 4 5 9 3 3 9 *